The Young Reader's Shakespeare
MACBETH

A Retelling by Adam McKeown

Illustrated by Lynne Cannoy

STERLING PUBLISHING CO., INC.
NEW YORK

IN MEMORY OF OUR DEVOTED EDITOR EXTRAORDINAIRE
SHEILA ANNE BARRY (1933–2003), WHO LOVED THE WITCHES IN *MACBETH*

———

WITH LOVE AND GRATITUDE TO KEITH, MOM AND TO THE MEMORY OF MY FATHER,
ELKIN, WHO WAS RIGHT AFTER ALL.   L.C.

———

Library of Congress Cataloging-In-Publication Data Available

2   4   6   8   10   9   7   5   3   1

Book Design by Deborah Kerner/Dancing Bears Design

Published by Sterling Publishing Co., Inc.
387 Park Avenue South, New York, NY 10016
Text © 2004 by Adam McKeown
Illustrations © 2004 by Lynne Cannoy
Distributed in Canada by Sterling Publishing
℅ Canadian Manda Group, 165 Dufferin Street
Toronto, Ontario, Canada M6K 3H6
Distributed in Great Britain and Europe by Chris Lloyd at Orca Book Services,
Stanley House, Fleets Lane, Poole BH15 3AJ, England
Distributed in Australia by Capricorn Link (Australia) Pty. Ltd.
P.O. Box 704, Windsor, NSW 2756, Australia

Printed in China
All rights reserved

Sterling ISBN 1-4027-2476-4

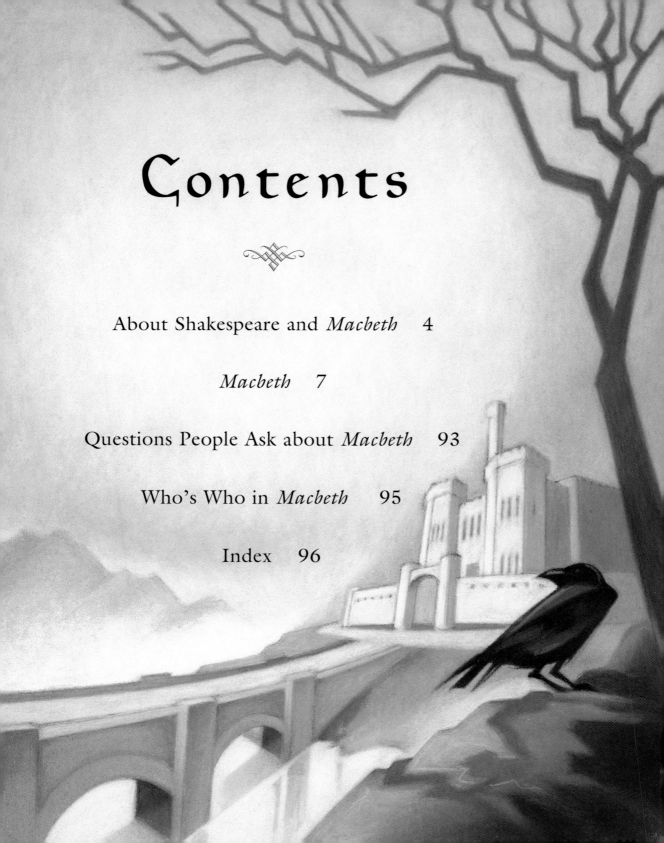

Contents

ABOUT SHAKESPEARE AND *MACBETH*

Macbeth, along with *Hamlet, Othello,* and *King Lear,* is considered one of Shakespeare's great tragedies, each written in the early 1600s when Shakespeare was around 40 years old. (He was born in 1564.) It is by far the strangest. Scholars are almost certain that he did not write all of it. It is the shortest of the four by a wide margin, and it seems to be missing important information. For example, readers have been wondering for centuries about Lady Macbeth's children. She mentions having at least one, but what happened to the child we are not told.

Although some scholars speculate that *Macbeth* was shortened for a traveling performance (perhaps when London playhouses were closed during plague outbreaks) or for a private performance, no one can say for sure. What is certain, however, is that the play, written probably around 1606, has a lot to do with the new king who took the throne in 1603.

The king was James VI and I (King James VI of Scotland and James I of England). When England's beloved queen, Elizabeth I, died childless in 1603, James, her distant cousin, became the rightful heir to the English throne. Unfortunately, Scotland and England had been at war for hundreds of years, and James's own mother, Mary Queen of Scots, had been killed on Elizabeth's orders. The people of England must have felt very uneasy about Scotland's king taking over their country. It was in this tense political climate that *Macbeth* was written.

In many ways, the play is a tribute to James, but an uneasy one. It celebrates the historical Banquo, the supposed founder of James's royal line. James was also a notoriously impatient theatergoer who did not care for long, inflated speeches, which might explain why *Macbeth* is so short and succinct. The witches in the play recall the notorious superstitions of James, who wrote a treatise on the dangers of witchcraft and aggressively prosecuted alleged witches. *Macbeth* is also full of powerful mother figures (Lady Macbeth, the witches, Hecate), a reminder perhaps that in becoming the king of both England and Scotland, James would finally lay to rest the rivalry between his mother and his mighty cousin, but only after both women were dead and much blood had been shed on both sides. For this reason, the play seems both optimistic about Great Britain, as the united kingdoms of England and Scotland were called, and haunted by the past.

To many people *Macbeth* is literally haunted—or, rather, cursed. According to one legend, the witches' famous "Double, double toil and trouble" speech (included here very nearly as it appears in the play) really was a magic spell through which sinister powers were able to gain control of the drama. Certainly this cannot be true, nor can it really be proven that productions of this play have met with any more accidents and calamities than any other play, but, according to legend, it has. Many people in the theater industry will not even utter the word *Macbeth* in the playhouse (except during the performance), and instead refer to it as "the Scottish play." I have said the word *Macbeth* in playhouses many times, and as yet nothing has happened to me. But if you are superstitious, you can do what many actors who utter the forbidden name do: leave the room, turn around thrice, spit over your shoulder, and then ask permission to reenter the room. (If you are caught spitting over your shoulder in your school theater, please don't tell the principal that you read about this practice here.)

The more you read *Macbeth*, the less you will concern yourself with whether the play is cursed and more with the reasons people like to imagine it is. As I mentioned, this play seems haunted. Each time you read it, you will be taken with a sense that the author has deliberately left information out, left stories only partially told. Just as Macbeth accuses the witches of being "imperfect speakers" (or incomplete speakers), the sense of something missing hangs over the play like a fog, and each time you read it, you will ask yourself what that something is, what hidden story is partially unfolding in the foggy intimations.

And each time the play gives only partial answers.

Chapter One

The wind moaned on the rain-battered heath. No sun or moon shone through the gloom, and nobody knew whether it was day or night.

On a lonely hilltop three witches held hands and turned in slow circles around a black cauldron. They chanted ancient and forgotten words, and with each flash of lighting, the cauldron bubbled and belched as if it were letting loose from its dismal muck one more demon or one more ghost to join the chorus of agonized voices crying in the wind.

Then, all of a sudden, they stopped, and when they did, the winds slackened and subsided. The lightning and the thunder moved on, leaving only a steady rain. Their work was done—at least for now.

"When shall we three meet again?" said one. "In thunder, lightning, or in rain?"

Another looked out into the darkness. "When the hurlyburly's done, when the battle's lost and won."

"Before the setting of the sun!" said the third, sniffing the air.

"Where?"

"On the heath."

"To meet Macbeth."

"Macbeth," they said in unison, and joined their bony hands once more. "Fair is foul and foul is fair," they chanted, "hover through the fog and filthy air!"

The cauldron began to bubble and smoke.

"Fair is foul!"

"And foul is fair!"

"Through the fog and
filthy air!"

A fireball rose from the cauldron
and exploded in the sky, turning
it an eerie green.

And when darkness returned,
the witches were gone.

Chapter Two

"Let him in!" Malcolm shouted.

The soldiers drew back the timber and turned the wheels that pulled the gates of the fortress open.

"Hurry!" said Malcolm. "He's dying!"

A lone soldier stumbled in and collapsed in the mud. Immediately the gates rumbled shut behind him.

"I come from . . ." He coughed. "From the front!"

"Take deep breaths," said Malcolm. "We need your intelligence—as soon as you can give it."

"What man is this?" Duncan, King of Scotland, peered out from a garret window of the inner fortress. He wore a suit of mail, although, for his own safety and the safety of the kingdom, he had not exposed himself to the hazards of the battle that had worn every man around him to the bone.

At the sound of the King's voice the man tried to raise himself on a knee.

"Save your strength for talking," said Malcolm. "Father, he has just come from . . ."

"Macbeth," the man said.

"Macbeth?" The king poked his head out a little further. "What about Macbeth?"

The man steadied himself.

"Speak!" said the King.

The soldiers drew close to the man to hear his words. Apprehension hung in the air as heavy as the storm. Were they about to be told Macbeth had been killed—along with their hopes of victory and peace?

"Long it stood undecided," said the man.

"And?"

"Father," said Malcolm. "Look at his wounds. Let him speak as he can."

"Like two exhausted swimmers," the man went on, his eyes far away, as if he were reliving the battle and not reporting it, "clinging to each other, pulling each other down. The armies of Macbeth and Macdonald. Until, like valor's firstborn son, Macbeth thrust himself into the thick of the battle, carving his way through the ranks, meeting the traitor man to man."

"The result!" shouted Duncan. His entire kingdom hung in the balance of Macbeth's campaign. If Macbeth had fallen, there was little hope left, and Duncan had to be ready to fight—or flee.

"Tell us plainly, good fellow," said Malcolm calmly, "whether Macbeth or Macdonald won."

The man stared at Malcolm as if he didn't know quite where he was or to whom he was speaking. "He was cut in half. With one stroke. From chin to belly button. Cut in half."

"Who?" said Malcolm.

"Macbeth . . ."

Silence fell.

"Macbeth. Cut him in half with one stroke."

"You mean, Macbeth won?" said Malcolm.

A murmur rose.

"Yes," the man said, finding strength in the joy his words were bringing. "And set the traitor's head on a pike."

"Praise heaven!" said Malcolm.

The man closed his eyes.

The murmur turned into laughter and then cheers.

Only then did the King venture out of the fortress. "Get this soldier to my surgeon!" he said, "and spread the news! Macbeth has won! Macbeth has defeated the traitorous Thane of Cawdor!"

But rumors flying faster than the words of kings went from the top of the battlements to the bottom of the walls, and the words "Macbeth!," "Peace!," and "Victory!" were passed from man to weary man.

"Send a message to Macbeth," said the King. "Go quickly. Say in the name of Duncan, King of Scotland, that the title forfeited by the traitor Macdonald now belongs to the man who valiantly rid our kingdom of him. Macbeth shall be Thane of Cawdor!"

The messenger saluted the King and rode off.

Chapter Three

"Where have you been, sister?" The witch removed a dead man's thumb from a pouch and kissed it before dropping it into the bubbling cauldron. Lightning tore through the sky as the ghastly thing sank into the broth.

Another witch stepped through the curtain of smoke.

"Killing swine. And you, sister?"

The third witch appeared on the spot where the lightning struck.

"Stealing chestnuts from a sailor's wife," she cackled. "'Begone, witch,' the prissy, pampered pullet said. But I know a thing or two about her husband."

"What, sister?"

"Tell."

"He's sailed off to Aleppo in a good ship called the *Tiger*. But in a sieve I'll thither sail and like a rat without a tail I'll do, I'll do, and I'll do!"

"I'll give you a wind." The hag raised her staff, and a gust blew out of the north.

Her companion made a sign and the wind began to howl in the east. "And I'll give you another."

"I myself have all the others!" said the third hag, lifting her hands as winds blew down from the south and west, driving the rain before them.

"Here I have a pilot's thumb," one of the witches said, stirring the cauldron, "wrecked as homeward he does come. He shall dwindle, peak, and pine!"

"Though his ship cannot be lost."

"Yet it shall be tempest tossed!"

Over the bellowing winds and the shrill laughter of the crones came a faint, steady beat.

"What's that, sister?"

"A drum?"

It beat more clearly now. A military drum, coming closer, marking time.

"A drum, a drum—Macbeth has come!"

In the deafening roar the three joined hands and chanted. "The weird sisters hand in hand, riders of the sea and land, thus do go about, about!"

And the sky began to turn with them. The clouds formed a cyclone that grew larger and more terrible as the witches counted out the circles they made.

"Thrice to thine!" said the first. Lighting erupted.

"And thrice to mine." The winds rose.

"And thrice again to make up nine!"

The sky heaved as the cyclone broke free like a wild horse.

Chapter Four

"So fair and foul a day I have not seen." Macbeth leaned into the wind, holding back the rain with his shield.

"I will take the fair for the foul," said Banquo, trudging behind Macbeth as the two made their way to a hilltop from which to survey the terrain before marching their soldiers on. "Give me victory in a storm over defeat in the sunshine any day!"

With their heads down and using all their strength to keep moving through the headwind, they didn't see the shadowy figures standing in the gloom until they had almost run into them.

"Ahhh!" Macbeth dropped his shield.

"Hail, Macbeth, Thane of Glamis," said the first.

"Hail, Macbeth, Thane of Cawdor," said the second.

"Hail, Macbeth," said the third, "who shall be king hereafter."

Their voices seemed to speak over the storm or beneath it, like a whisper in the ear or an echo inside a deep cauldron.

"All hail!" they said.

Banquo stepped in front of his startled friend and drew his sword. "Are you creatures of this world or some other?" he said. "Are you living or dead? Speak!"

"Hail noble Banquo," said the first hag, "lesser than Macbeth and yet greater."

"Hail noble Banquo," said the second, "less fortunate than Macbeth but more so."

"Hail Banquo," said the third, "who shall never be king but will father them."

"All hail."

The hags stood there, staring and grinning from beneath their hoods.

Macbeth, still reeling from his fright, tried to make sense of the strange words he had heard. Thane of Cawdor? King? What could it mean? He needed to know more.

"Wait," he said. "I am Thane of Glamis, yes, but I am not in line to be Thane of Cawdor. And to be king? I could never dream it, let alone believe it."

As he spoke, the witches vanished.

Macbeth whirled around. "Come back! Come back and explain!"

"The earth has bubbles as the water has."

Banquo handed Macbeth his shield. "Were those things real or was there something wrong with the bread we ate?"

But Macbeth was not able to laugh. "Cawdor? King? How? Why? Why tell us only half of what we need to know?"

"I don't see why you should fear things that sound so fair. To be the Thane of Cawdor wouldn't be so bad—and Cawdor doesn't have a thane at the moment—since you stuck his head on a pike just now. And, personally, I think you'd make a good king. Cheer up." Banquo slapped Macbeth on the shoulder. "I'm the one who should be worried. I'll be looking up at you my whole life, though I suppose being father to a king should be quite a comfort to a dead man!"

"What do you mean I'd make a good king?" said Macbeth. "We have a good king, and I don't aspire to take his place. I'm Thane of Glamis. That is enough for any man. It is all I am and all I should hope for."

"I meant nothing by it, though one may say a man would make a good king without being a traitor. One may even believe it himself without hoping for it. Right?"

"Yes." Macbeth slung his shield over his shoulder. The winds had subsided a bit, but the rain still fell steadily. "Of course, but those are dangerous words. All my life I have tried to be valiant but not ambitious. Ambitious thanes make kings uneasy. I would not want the King to know those words were spoken— I wouldn't want him to think they were mine."

"Don't worry about it. You and I were the only ones who heard them, and I won't tell anyone."

"Good."

"Right."

Macbeth paused. "And I hope it isn't true."

"Me too," said Banquo. "Who wants to be king? Always having to keep a watchful eye on the most noble and powerful thanes, always having to fear those most able to serve? Not me. I wouldn't even want my great-great-grand-nephew twice removed to be a king. Thane of Cawdor maybe—"

"Not even!" said Macbeth.

"Make way!" came a voice from the ranks of soldiers at the bottom of the hill.

"What's this?" said Macbeth.

"A messenger from the King," said Banquo, "looks like. Probably here to offer a word of thanks in exchange for saving his realm!"

The messenger galloped forward and dismounted. "My Lord," he said.

"Greetings," said Macbeth. "Stand at ease and tell us your news."

"My Lord," he said. "As a reward for the service you have performed today, Duncan, King of Scotland, declares that you shall be hereafter Thane of Cawdor and shall enjoy all lands and rights pertaining . . ."

"What?"

"Thane of Cawdor, my Lord. Macbeth is Thane of Cawdor."

"Can this be?" said Banquo. He read the decree and looked at his friend.

"Leave us," said Macbeth.

The messenger bowed and departed.

Macbeth stared out on the stormy heath long after the horse and rider had disappeared. "And so it is true, what these hags have said."

"Partially," said Banquo, "but remember it is the way of evil people to predict one quite possible thing and two or three impossible things in the same breath. That way, when the first comes true—as it was likely to anyway—a man drives himself mad anticipating the rest, or trying to bring it to pass. Surely that's what these weird sisters had in mind when they hailed us."

"But now I am Thane of Cawdor, just as they said."

"And you were likely to be. Macdonald was a traitor and you slew him—valiantly. By Scottish law his title and lands are the king's to dispose of. Who if not you should be Thane of Cawdor now?"

"Yes." Macbeth tried to make light of it. "Yes, of course. But I would think you'd hope they were telling the truth. They said you will be the father of kings."

"But that should make you unhappy," said Banquo, "for if they were telling the truth then you will be king, and therefore you stand in the way of my children's hopes."

The two men looked at each other for a while until, finally, Banquo spoke.

"I'll tell you what," he said, "if you should be king I promise I won't try to kill you, if you don't try to kill my children."

"Agreed." Macbeth smiled. "If I should become king it will be because of chance and not these strange predictions. So fear not. Let's speak no more of it."

Chapter Five

Deep in her inmost chamber Lady Macbeth sat by candlelight. On her table was a letter she had read many, many times.

It came from her husband.

She had all but memorized the words and had been, for hours, arranging and rearranging them in her head, trying to decide what they meant.

Surely, the creatures her husband described were no ordinary mortals. They were witches, and the words of witches were not to be taken lightly. But her husband, of course, had taken them lightly, or so it seemed to her.

"And they said I will be king," her husband wrote. The words scrolled across her memory.

Lady Macbeth grew more and more feverish. She thought: That was so like him. He was not one to listen to what people were really saying or to seize opportunities. Three witches told him he would be Thane of Cawdor—and now he is. They also told him that he would be king. But he presents it like so much ordinary news, as if becoming king lay not in his power or his hope. All he needs is a sword and the will to use it!

He was too full of the milk of human kindness to take advantage of situations. Lady Macbeth drummed her fingers on the table, thinking. But is it really kindness to sit back and let others snatch what they want while leaving your own future to chance? If I were a man, I think I would not let such momentous opportunities pass me by. Come home, my husband. I will pour my spirits in your ear and whip you with the valor of my words, so that nothing will impede you from the greatness the Fates have decreed.

At the door came a faint knocking.

"Who is it?"

"Madam," one of Lady Macbeth's waiting women poked her head through the door. "There is a messenger. The King is coming here tonight with his sons and my lord Macbeth, and Banquo, too."

"Thank you," said Lady Macbeth. "Make ready for them."

The door closed.

Lady Macbeth stood and walked to the win-

dow. The storm continued to batter the bleak hills, but it pleased her. She liked the chill of storms, the sound of winds, the coal-black ravens riding updrafts on shaggy outstretched wings. It energized her.

The raven himself is hoarse, she thought, that croaks the fatal entrance of Duncan under my battlements.

She vowed then that the King would never leave her castle alive.

She shuddered, half in delight and half in fear.

"Come," she whispered into the storm. "Come you spirits that tend on mortal thoughts. Transform me. Fill me from crown to toe with direst cruelty. Make thick my blood. Come to my woman's body, you murdering ministers, and take away care and tenderness and every other thing that becomes a woman. Let nothing shake my foul purpose. Let my keen knife see not the wound it makes, nor heaven peep through the blanket of the dark to cry, 'Hold, hold!'"

Chapter Six

Duncan and his sons, Malcolm and Donalbain, rode with Banquo and his son Fleance. All were in good spirits as their horses clomped up the steep path that led to Inverness Castle. The war was over, the rebellion put down, and even the sky seemed to brighten a bit. Now was the time for celebration and friends.

Macbeth, riding on ahead of them, was less at ease. He was happy to be coming home, but the words of the strange women still vexed him. He almost wished he hadn't written to his wife about them. She was bound to get agitated, especially since the prediction echoed something she had told him many times: "You are a better man than Macdonald and ought to be Thane of Cawdor. You are the most valiant man in the kingdom and ought to be Duncan's successor." If he had a penny for every time he'd heard it, he could buy a kingdom and not have to worry about killing anyone to get it.

He almost stopped his horse dead in its tracks. Now why did you think a thing like that, Macbeth? Who said anything about killing? You are a subject of the King, not a rival, and not a killer.

But that was a lie. He had just killed a hundred men in the battle against Macdonald. Killing had become—did he dare think it?—easy. More than once since he met the witches it had crossed his mind—mostly as an idle fantasy, though— that he would need kill only one more to make the pre- diction come true.

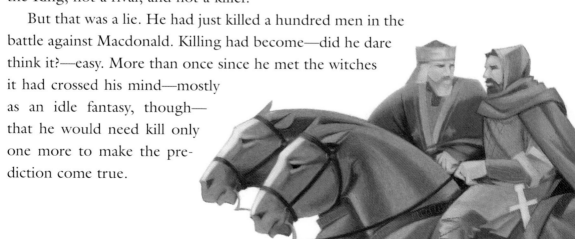

And this fact certainly would have occurred to his wife.

"What's wrong there, cousin?" said Duncan, riding up beside him.

"Nothing, my liege. Just pleased to see Inverness again."

"As am I. I was just telling Banquo how fond I am of this place. The sweetness of the air is made sweeter by the song of the martin, even in winter."

The gate at Inverness stood open for Macbeth and his royal guests. As they rode through, the soldiers lowered their swords in salute, the kettle drummers signaled to the trumpeters on the battlements, and the people in the castle poured out of the buildings to greet the returning heroes with a rousing cheer.

Duncan waved to the crowd, dismounted, and ascended a stair. The people shouted. Duncan raised his hand and began to speak. "As you know the battle lost and won—lost by the traitor Macdonald and won by us—has saved Scotland. And now that is in the past, it is time to think about the future. By custom, a Scottish king must choose a successor from among those worthiest to govern this land. If only there were Scotland enough to bestow on those worthy. Banquo, come forward."

The crowd parted to let Banquo approach the King. Duncan said, "You deserve no less praise and reward than any. Know, noble Banquo, that you shall always be as near my heart as my own family."

"You too, Fleance," Duncan said to Banquo's son.

"I only hope to serve you as loyally." Banquo bowed.

"And now Macbeth," said Duncan. "Everyone here has heard the stories by now, but the stories cannot do justice to the truth. Listen."

The crowd was silent.

"The man you called Thane of Glamis," said the King, "proved himself to be Scotland's bravest champion, dismantling Macdonald's army and beheading the traitor himself. For this he returns to you bearing the title most coveted by the Scottish peers, Thane of Cawdor!"

"Hooray!" shouted the crowd. "Hail, Thane of Cawdor!"

"It is an honor I hope I can live up to," Macbeth said, but in his heart he was confused. Hadn't Duncan praised him as Scotland's bravest champion?

Shouldn't he then be the successor? Perhaps the King was trying to build suspense.

Lady Macbeth's cold fingers gripped her husband's hand.

"But there is more." Duncan quieted the crowd with a wave. "There is no better place to pronounce this last decision than here at Inverness, in the home of our greatest defender and his most gracious lady." He cleared his throat.

Macbeth trembled at the words. His doubts of a moment before were replaced with anticipation. Yes, he thought, I am Scotland's greatest protector—I have always been—and now I will become the successor to her throne. It is an honor I dreamt not of, he said to himself, as if the pronouncement had already been made.

"Sons, kinsmen, thanes," said Duncan, "and you who are closest to me and them, know we will establish our estate upon our eldest son, Malcolm, whom we name hereafter the Prince of Cumberland, successor to our throne. This is an honor not for him alone but for all of you. Revere him as your prince and let his nobility, like stars, shine back on you."

A hush fell as Malcolm came forward and bowed to his father.

Macbeth was stunned. For a terrifying moment he hated Duncan and Malcolm, as if the two had conspired to rob him of something that truly belonged to him. But he checked himself. It was the witches' prophecy working its evil on him. Fight it, he told himself, fight it. If you are indeed worthy of the throne, then you should be big enough to accept that it shall not be yours.

"Long live the King!" cried Banquo, breaking the silence.

The crowd followed Banquo's lead, shouting "Long live the King!" and "Long live the Prince of Cumberland!"

But Macbeth couldn't cheer. Try as he might to tell himself that the throne was not his, that Duncan was a fine king and Malcolm a worthy prince, the words "Long live the King!" and "Long live the Prince of Cumberland!" stuck in his throat. It grieved him to admit it, but—at this moment anyway—he did not want either of them to live long.

Lady Macbeth put her arm around him, as if she read his mind.

Chapter Seven

Lady Macbeth slipped silently into her husband's chamber, but once the door was closed she said, "Hail, Macbeth, Thane of Cawdor."

Macbeth whirled and faced her. "Those are the witches' words. Why do you say them?"

"Because I cannot yet call you king." She drifted toward her husband. "Your letters have transported me beyond this ignorant present," she said, "and I feel now the future in the instant."

"What do you mean?"

"What are Duncan's plans?"

"To celebrate with us tonight and leave tomorrow, as he pleases. Why?" But Macbeth knew the answer already.

"Oh, never shall sun that morrow see!"

"Quiet!" Macbeth's heart beat faster. He tiptoed to the door and put his ear against it, as though someone might be listening.

"There is no one to hear except your own ambitions," Lady Macbeth said.

Macbeth unlaced his armor. "We will talk more of this later."

"There will be no later if it is not now."

"Well, what would you have me do?!"

"I would have you be subtle," Lady Macbeth said, sliding up to her husband's side. "I would have you bear welcome in your eye, your hand, your tongue. Look like the innocent flower, but be the serpent under it."

Macbeth took deep breaths to calm himself. It didn't do any good. "We . . . will talk more of this . . . later."

Lady Macbeth jerked away as if she had been stung. "Will you forfeit a title to a lesser man?"

"I didn't say that!"

"Then what do you say? Do you not see that the time to act is now? Do you not see that the kingdom stands within your grasp? Do you not see that one small stroke of the blade stands between you and the throne you deserve? Between Scotland and the king she deserves? Do you not see?"

"I see all that!" Macbeth said.

Lady Macbeth raised an eyebrow. "Then you will take action? You will swear to it?"

Macbeth could see his wife would not leave him alone without getting the answer she wanted, and yet he could not commit to a deed he could scarcely think about. "There will be action in time."

Lady Macbeth went to the door. "In time?" she said. "I will hold you to your promise."

She closed the door silently behind her.

Chapter Eight

Alone Macbeth paced around his chamber. His wife had said nothing that he had not thought himself. Were murdering Duncan the be-all and end-all here and now—on this bank and shoal of time—without any consequences in this world or the world to come, it would be a simple matter. Of course, he would kill him. But there would be consequences. If he were caught . . . but it was more than that.

Even if he were not caught, the murder would destroy him. Bloody instructions return to plague their inventor, and even-handed justice always finds a way to bring the poisoned chalice back to our own lips. Duncan was there in double trust: First Macbeth was a kinsman and a subject, second, he was a host—one who should shut the door against a murderer, not be one himself. Besides, Duncan had been so gentle and good a king that his virtues would plead like angels against the murder. And if Macbeth were to kill him anyway, surely pity—like a newborn babe—would blow the horrid deed in every eye so that tears would drown the wind. No. No good would come from killing Duncan. It would be a wound too deep for Scotland to bear, a crime too foul for Macbeth's conscience to bear. It was a price too high for ambition.

Chapter Nine

The servants hurried back from the kitchen with trenchers full of meats and dainties. Legs of lamb, sausages, mince pies, baked apples, candied pears, sugar loaves—the guests consumed it all nearly as quickly as it hit the table.

Macbeth did his best to put on a good face amidst the laughter and the clanking of cups, but he didn't feel any of the joy with which his hall resounded. He could scarcely look at Duncan and Malcolm without feeling cheated. And this feeling made him a shallow, greedy, ungrateful monster in his own eyes. Unable to bear what his desires had turned him into, and certain someone would notice, he withdrew to the kitchen on the pretext of making sure food and drink were in good supply.

Lady Macbeth followed him. "He has almost eaten and drunk his fill. Soon he will be asleep in bed."

"We will proceed no further in this business," Macbeth spoke without looking his wife in the eyes. "He has honored me of late, and I have bought golden opinions from all sorts of people. I think it would be best to enjoy what I have been freely given rather than risk throwing away all I have."

Lady Macbeth frowned. "Are you afraid to let your actions be as bold as your desires? Would you be content with the honors and opinions of others but to live a coward in your own esteem?"

"Peace!" Macbeth knew she was trying to stoke his passions. He vowed not to let her. "I dare do all that may become a man. Any man who dares do more is none."

"When you had the courage to do it, then you were a man." Lady Macbeth circled around him. "Tell me, what beast was it then that made you break this enterprise to me?"

"You are my wife. I tell you all."

"But we don't just speak without hoping our words have some effect. Why did you tell me the prophecy if you did not cherish the thought of being king?"

"Just because I cherish the thought does not mean I would will it into existence."

"But you do cherish it?" Lady Macbeth pursued him. "And all it lacks is the will, for the ability you have. Think of it. You could be king, if you only had more confidence in yourself."

"I have confidence."

"Once I thought you did."

"Do you think it is so easy to kill an innocent man?"

"I have nursed a baby," Lady Macbeth said, "and I would, even while it was smiling in my face, have dashed out its brains if I had sworn to do it, as you have sworn to do this!"

"I swore because you could not be satisfied otherwise."

"You swore because you want to be king and for no other reason!"

Macbeth could not argue. He was Thane of Cawdor because he killed Macdonald. What was the difference between killing an enemy to gain favor and killing someone else for some other reason?

"What if we fail?" It was not the question Macbeth intended to ask.

Lady Macbeth smiled. "We fail? But screw your courage to the sticking place, and we'll not fail! When Duncan is asleep, I will drug his attendants and lay their weapons out for you. When the clock strikes one, you'll kill Duncan with their swords and smear them with his blood. They will be blamed—and no one would believe us capable of this crime. No one will suspect us. No one will deter us. No one will catch us."

Macbeth's mind was in turmoil. His wife was right. Killing the King and deflecting the blame onto his foolish bodyguards would be easy. He had killed more men than he could count, but his reputation was spotless. No one would take the word of a guard over his. One little action, one little stroke of the dagger, was all that stood between him and the kingdom.

"Then you are resolved to do it?" said Lady Macbeth, breaking the silence.

Was he? Macbeth nodded, reluctant to say the words.

Lady Macbeth wanted a clearer answer. "Are you resolved?"

"Resolved." Macbeth nodded.

Chapter Ten

The party wound down once Duncan went to bed. Only a handful of revelers lingered at the tables as the servants cleaned up around them. Fleance stretched and went to look for his father.

He found him on the balcony, staring out upon the gloomy heath.

"How goes the night, boy?" said Banquo.

"The moon is down," said Fleance. "It is very late."

"The heavens are thrifty tonight. Their candles are all out." Banquo handed his belt and dagger to his son. "Take these."

"Why, sir?"

"Sometimes a man cannot rest unless he knows his children are safe."

"These are fears that come upon us when we are tired. There is no safer place than Inverness. Won't you go to bed?"

"Fatigue lies like lead upon me, but horrible visions have come to me of late in dreams. I don't want to sleep."

A shadow fell across the light from the doorway behind.

"Who's there?" said Banquo.

It was Macbeth. "A friend."

"What, sir, not yet at rest?" Banquo said. "The King's already in bed."

"Is he? I hadn't noticed." But of course he had. "Why aren't you?"

"I dreamt last night of the three weird sisters. To you they have shown some truth."

"I think not of them."

"No?"

"No. And yet . . ." Macbeth came to Banquo's side and lowered his voice. "When there is time I would talk with you about that business."

"I am here at your leisure."

"If . . ." Macbeth chose his words very carefully, concealing his meaning so that he would be able to deny it later, if it came to that. "If you were . . . to stand by me—if the issue arose—that is . . . if there were ever a question of who should be king . . . there would be honor for you."

Banquo turned and faced Macbeth. "So long as I lose no honor in seeking it."

"Yes. Certainly," said Macbeth. "Certainly. I only meant that . . . one never knows who will oppose Duncan's choice . . . should Duncan . . . should anything happen." Macbeth laughed. "Heh-heh. Look, we defended this kingdom once before—you and I—and we should stand by each other if we ever have to do so again. That's all I meant."

"Heh-heh. Yes." Banquo knew that wasn't what Macbeth meant. "You can count on that."

"Right!" said Macbeth. "Now, get some rest."

"You too, friend," said Banquo.

Macbeth left.

Banquo drew his sword and gave it to Fleance. "You'd better take this, too."

Chapter Eleven

When at last everyone had gone to bed, Macbeth walked alone in the long, cold corridors of his castle, thinking about the murder. One little cut, he thought. That's all. It isn't much. Not much. It wouldn't be the first time in the history of the world a kingdom had been won with a murder. It is a small thing.

He waited for the sound of the bell. He wanted to feel the cold resolve spread through his veins. But the waiting made that one little murder seem so big. If it were done when 'tis done, then 'twere well it were done quickly, he thought.

He walked faster down the dark hallway, trying not to think about the deed, waiting for the clock to strike one.

"Hooo!" cried an owl.

Macbeth leapt out of his skin. His dagger clattered against the stone floor.

He fumbled in the darkness for it. Just an owl, he told himself. Just an owl. Pick up your weapon. Pick it up. But where was it?

Then he saw it.

The dagger.

It was floating in the air.

His eyes widened. His lips trembled. "Is this a dagger which I see before me, the handle toward my hand?" He didn't know whether he was thinking the words or speaking them out loud. "Come! Let me clutch thee!"

He reached for the dagger but his hands passed through it.

"I have thee not, and yet I see thee still. Are you not, fatal vision, as sensible to feeling as to sight? Or are you but a dagger of the mind?"

The dagger began to drift away. Macbeth followed it, stepping on his own dagger as he did so.

"I see you yet, in form as palpable as this which I now draw."

Macbeth picked his dagger up and wrapped his fingers comfortably around the sturdy handle.

The dagger continued to drift away, toward the staircase that led to the bedroom where Duncan lay.

"You lead me the way that I was going!"

The cool thrill of resolution came over Macbeth, the same intent he felt when he lifted his sword to cut Macdonald in two. Yes. How wondrous. How marvelous. While half the world goes about its business, this half sleeps, insensible to the crimes of night. He felt invisible, made of air. Terror pulled at him, but it became part of the strange power that spurred him forward. Yes. This is the moment. Courage and fear blurred into one profound emotion. And there was the dagger, leading him on.

His foot touched the stair.

And then the clock struck one.

Chapter Twelve

Lady Macbeth sat in darkness, thinking about what was done and what was yet to be done. She had drugged the guards on schedule. Now they slept as if they were dead. All that remained was the crime itself, but this she could not control.

How long had it been since the clock struck? she wondered. Too long.

She stood and began to pace.

Maybe the guards woke up—maybe the dose had not been strong enough. No. She had mixed it herself. Or perhaps her husband did not find the guards' weapons. No. He could not miss them. Then what? Was her husband too soft-hearted?

I should have done it myself, she thought, and I would have except . . . except, sleeping there so peacefully, Duncan reminded me of my own father. A wave of guilt came over her, but she fought it off. It has to be done, she told herself. We deserve the kingdom. It is not so much a murder as a correction. But where was Macbeth?

She didn't have to wait any longer. "My husband," she said.

"I have done the deed." Macbeth staggered into the bedroom, his face and shirt covered with Duncan's blood. "I . . ." He froze. "Did you hear a noise?"

"I heard the owl scream and the crickets cry. Did you not speak?"

"When?"

"Now."

"As I came in?"

"Yes."

"Shhh." Macbeth put his ear to the wall. "Who lies in this room?"

"Donalbain."

Lady Macbeth lit a candle.

Only then did Macbeth see the blood. "This is a sorry sight," he said, looking at his hands.

"It's a foolish thing to say 'a sorry sight.'"

Macbeth slumped into a chair. "One laughed in his sleep and the other cried 'murder.' They woke each other up, the fools. But they said their prayers and went back to sleep. Funny." Macbeth smiled joylessly. "When they said 'God bless us,' I could not say 'Amen.'"

"Don't think about it," said Lady Macbeth, wiping her husband's face with a handkerchief.

"But why could I not say 'Amen'?" Macbeth spoke as if in a trance. "I had most need of blessing, but 'Amen' stuck in my throat."

"You must not think this way. Things without all remedy should be without regard. What's done is done."

"And then I thought I heard a voice cry, 'Sleep no more! Macbeth does murder sleep.' The innocent sleep." Macbeth's eyes were wide, fixed on the flickering candlelight. "Sleep that knits up the raveled sleeve of care."

Lady Macbeth shook her husband. "What do you mean?"

"The voice cried, 'Sleep no more. Glamis has murdered sleep and therefore Cawdor shall sleep no more! Macbeth shall sleep no more.'"

"Who was it who cried? Who? Nobody. Drink some water. Wash . . ."

Then she saw the bloody daggers still in Macbeth's belt.

"Why did you bring these here!? They have to be found near the body. You must go back at once and leave them and smear the guards with blood."

"I'll go no more. I am afraid to think what I have done. I dare not look on it again."

Lady Macbeth knew then that if the plan were to be successful it was going to be up to her. She stood. "Give me the daggers," she said and then chided her husband. "Infirm of purpose! The sleeping and the dead are but as pictures. It is the eye of childhood that fears them."

She hurried out of the bedroom.

Macbeth didn't notice she had left—or didn't care. "What is that sound? Huh. Why does every noise frighten me?" He lowered his head to his hands but jerked away. "What hands are these? Ah, they pluck out my eyes!" He stared at the drying blood that ringed each fingernail and etched red-brown lines in every pore and wrinkle.

Lady Macbeth returned, her bare arms covered with blood. "My hands are now of your color, but I would be ashamed to wear a heart so white."

There was a loud knocking at the south entry gate.

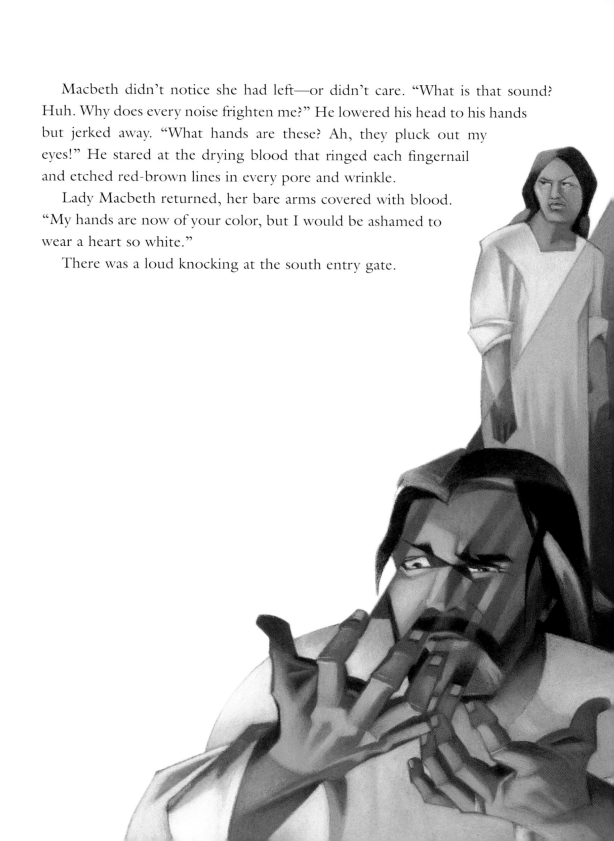

Chapter Thirteen

Outside Inverness Castle, Macduff, the Thane of Fife, waited in the driving rain for the doors to open. With him was Lennox, one of Duncan's most trusted lords.

"Knock again," said Macduff.

Lennox pounded on the heavy oaken gates with the hilt of his sword.

Macduff pulled his cloak up around his ears.

Lennox was about to knock again when the doors opened.

"Didn't you hear us knocking?!" Macduff shouted at the face that appeared in the light, until he saw at whom he was yelling. "Great thane! Forgive me."

"No matter," said Macbeth nervously. "The porter is sleeping soundly—it was a long night of celebration. Come in."

"It was a long night for us, too," said Lennox.

"Oh?"

"Yes." Macduff peeled off his wet jacket. "Forgive my rudeness, Macbeth, but I have urgent news for the King. He hasn't left yet, has he?"

"The King?" said Macbeth. "No. He's asleep. In the west bedroom. You'll find him there."

"By your leave," said Macduff.

"Of course."

Macduff went upstairs.

"So," said Macbeth to Lennox, "you say it was a long night?"

"Yes." Lennox shivered. "Unruly. Where we lay our chimneys were blown down. And they say laments were heard in the air—strange screams of death and prophesying with accents terrible, of dire combustion and confused events

newly hatched to the woeful time. The owl clamored all night long, and the earth was feverous and did shake."

"A rough night."

"Yes." It was an unnerving understatement. "They say Duncan's horses, the pride of the kingdom, broke loose and turned wild."

"Wild?"

"And ate each other."

"Think of that. Heh-heh."

Macbeth's nervous distraction was starting to worry Lennox.

"So," said Macbeth.

"May I come in and warm up?" said Lennox.

"Oh. Certainly. You must be cold."

"Indeed."

"Horror! Horror! Horror!" shouted Macduff, bounding down the stairs.

"Murder! Murder has stolen the life from the castle!"

Chapter Fourteen

"What?" said Macbeth stupidly. "The life?"

"You mean His Majesty?" said Lennox.

"Come to the chamber," said Macduff. "See for yourselves. Don't make me speak it!"

They all ran up the stairs. There was a pause—and then confused shouts. An alarm bell rang. More shouts. Voices calling "Murder!" Others yelling "Seal the doors!" And then men screaming. Bloody, gagging screams of agony and death.

Lady Macbeth flew out of her bedroom and met Macduff in the hallway.

"What's the matter?" she said.

"Gentle lady, it is not for you to hear what I would speak," he said.

Banquo joined them. "What is it?"

Macduff's eyes darted from Lady Macbeth to Banquo. "The King," he said. "Murdered."

"What? In our house?" Lady Macbeth swayed and gasped.

Banquo steadied her, just as Malcolm and Donalbain arrived.

"What's wrong?" said Donalbain.

Macbeth stepped slowly out of the bedroom, his arms bloody. Lennox followed, an expression of terror on his face.

"Will someone tell us what's amiss?!" said Malcolm.

"You are," said Macbeth. "The fountain of your blood is stopped."

"Your royal father is murdered," said Macduff.

"By whom?"

"By his guards," Lennox said, casting a glance back at the grizzly scene in the bedroom and another at Macbeth. "Or so it seems. There were bloody daggers by the pillows. On which the guards slept. Quite soundly. Until Macbeth . . . killed them."

"Oh, yet I do repent my fury," said Macbeth.

"What?" Macduff was staggered. "Why did you do it?"

Macbeth threw up his hands. "Who can be wise, amazed, temperate, furious, loyal, and neutral at the same time? My love for Duncan got the best of me."

Macduff stared at Macbeth, not sure what to make of his explanation. "Still we must inquire further into these deeds. The guards would not have acted on their own."

"Yes," said Macbeth. "Quickly, let us meet in the main hall. Malcolm and Donalbain, stay close by us. You are not safe until we have dug up this treachery by its roots."

Macbeth went downstairs, followed by Macduff and Lennox. Malcolm and Donalbain remained behind.

"The guards?" said Donalbain. "I doubt that."

"Let's not consort with them," said Malcolm.

"The arrow that killed our father has not yet landed. We should get out of here now."

"Where will you go?"

"To England," said Malcolm. "You go to Ireland. It will be harder to kill us both that way."

There was no time for grief. The two brothers knew that whoever killed their father did so not to kill a man but to kill a king. And that meant he would also kill a king's sons.

And they knew that whoever the murderer was, he was still at Inverness.

Chapter Fifteen

It wasn't much of a morning, if it *was* morning. Banquo slept little during the night, sitting in a chair by Fleance's bed, watching over him. At some point he must have drifted off, but he didn't know when. And now it was day, but a day without sun. He didn't think it possible for storm clouds to be as black as midnight, but the world was proving itself to be full of horrible surprises. He stood on the battlements pondering the thickness of the gloom when he was joined by Macduff.

"Macbeth is preparing to go to Scone to be made King."

"Already?" said Banquo.

"Yes," said Macduff. "The sudden departure of Malcolm and Donalbain convinced the peers that they were behind their father's murder. They have been condemned as traitors and stripped of their titles."

"Lucky the guards are not alive to refute that conviction." Banquo kicked fretfully at the stone walls. "I shouldn't have said that. These are dangerous days."

"They are."

"And so Macbeth is King," said Banquo. "Was it his own suggestion?"

Macduff did not answer.

"Will you go to Scone to celebrate his good fortune?" said Banquo.

"No," said Macduff. "I will go back to Fife. I . . . I can't explain. I need to know that my wife and children are safe."

"I understand."

But Macduff didn't leave. "And then—"

"And then?"

41

"And then I will go to England. I am told by one I trust . . ." Macduff looked around. ". . . the Prince has fled there. I will encourage him to come back. I fear Macbeth—"

"Don't say it." Banquo understood. "But what about your family? When the murderer . . . when the King . . . learns you went to assist Malcolm, he will—"

"None of us is safe while a tyrant reigns. What I do for Scotland I do for my family, but . . ." Macduff closed his eyes, "Will you look to their safety while I am gone?"

"With all my power," said Banquo. "Good luck."

Macduff left.

In the whorls of fog twisting in the wind on the barren heaths, Banquo could almost imagine the faces of the dead and hear their moans in the wind. It was all wrong—Duncan's death. Even the sky knew it.

Well, Macbeth, Banquo thought, you have it now: kingdom, Cawdor, Glamis, all, just as the witches promised. And I fear you have played most foully for it. Yet they also said the kingdom will not pass to your children but to mine.

"So it has come to placing our hopes in the words of witches," said Banquo. "Heaven help us all."

"Here he is," said Macbeth in a big voice, coming up the stairs to the battlements. "Keeping watch, eh?"

"We feared you had slipped out in the night to hunt down the traitors," said Lady Macbeth, coming up behind. "And then what kind of party would we have?"

"Party?" said Banquo glumly.

"Yes," said Macbeth, "we are moving the royal court to Dunsinane, and we thought we would warm that venerable castle with a party. At which I hoped you would be our chief guest."

Dunsinane? Banquo thought. It was more of a bunker than a castle. An old and ghastly block of limestone built on a hilltop centuries ago to repel Vikings, it had served the kings of Scotland as a last desperate refuge. Hardly a place for a royal court—or a party.

"It should be grand," said Banquo.

"I would ask you to come with us to Scone," said Macbeth, "but sadly I must call on you to ride out and gather information about Malcolm and Donalbain. Some say they have gone to England and others say to Ireland. We need to know."

"I will ride out, Your Highness."

"And you will take Fleance with you?" said Macbeth.

Banquo saw at that moment the plan taking shape in Macbeth's twisted brain. If he and Fleance rode together they could both be killed without its seeming too neat a coincidence. After all, if Macbeth would kill Duncan to gain a kingdom, he would certainly kill lesser men to keep it.

"Lost in thought?" said Macbeth.

"I was just considering, Your Highness. Might it not be best for Fleance and I to split up? That way he could follow one fugitive and I the other?"

"Too risky," said Macbeth.

"No risk is too great in your protection."

"Nonsense," said Macbeth, "I won't think of it. You and your son are the jewels of my crown. Stay with him until these traitors are found."

"Very well, Your Highness. I will see you then at Dunsinane."

"We count on it."

Banquo bowed and trudged down the stairs, quite sure—though he told himself to be hopeful—he wouldn't live to see Macbeth again.

Chapter Sixteen

Banquo's cool reticence did not go unnoticed by Macbeth. "He suspects."

All the pleasure and confidence that came with kingship drained away. To be king is nothing, he thought, but to be safely king! Our fears in Banquo stick deep, and his royal nature ought to be feared—the dauntless temper of his mind, the wisdom that guides his valor. His kingly bearing undermines my kingship every minute he lives.

He remembered how Banquo reacted to the witches' prophecy—as if being father to a line of kings meant nothing. How noble!

It made him sick.

In his imagination Macbeth saw the Scottish people cheering for Banquo, just as they once cheered for him. And now? Everyone knew he was a murderer, even if they were afraid to say it, and soon they would praise the stars that made sure he had no children of his own to inherit the iron rod of tyranny. It grieved him to the core of his soul, and he wished he could make time go backward. How much happier was that day when he was made Thane of Cawdor, a good king's most trusted general, champion of a proud and free Scotland, and not a murderer, a liar, and a thief!

But time doesn't go backward. What's done is done. The best anyone can do is make the most of the situation. He was King—regardless of how or why. He had to think ahead now.

"You called for us, Your Majesty?" A lean, weather-beaten man came up the stairs. He was followed by another, whose face was concealed under a dark hood.

"Come," said Macbeth. "It is time for the business we discussed. Today the general Banquo and his son Fleance will ride forth. It is for them that I have hired you."

"For Banquo?" said the man.

"Aye," said Macbeth. "Banquo. And his son. You will be well paid."

Chapter Seventeen

The castle guard turned around on some pretense five miles back. Banquo and Fleance rode alone. They could barely see twenty feet in front of them, so thick was the fog and murk.

"Isn't it strange that we should be searching for these traitors alone, Father?"

Not so strange, thought Banquo. How else will Macbeth be able to murder us? Banquo tried his best to put on a good face for his son.

"The King trusts us," said Banquo. "He thinks you and I should do the work of ten men. You do have your sword and dagger about you?"

"Yes, Father. For the tenth time, yes."

"Better I should annoy you with questions than fail in my duty as your father to safeguard your person."

"You've been very solicitous about my person, sir," said Fleance. "I should think I was the safest man in Scotland, riding out armed beside the most stalwart general in the kingdom."

"Keep that sense of humor about you," said Banquo, smiling. "It will be a faithful companion in the years to come. But remember that your father is just an ordinary man."

"Who likes to worry!"

"I will make a deal with you then," said Banquo. "If you promise me you will be safe, I will keep my worries to myself."

"Yes, Father."

"I mean that. If anything should happen, don't bother with me. Protect yourself. Flee. Ride home. Don't look back."

Fleance knew his father well. A military man, Banquo was always thinking about physical security, always thinking about threats, always mapping out escape routes and rallying points. Fleance didn't pay much attention to what he understood as his father's habitual paranoia. "I won't. If you so much as sneeze, I will bolt. You will rejoice in my cowardice. I promise."

"Good," said Banquo. "You make me proud. Now let's pick up the pace."

They spurred their horses to a gallop and rode single file. In the dense fog the sound traveled nowhere, creating the eerie sensation that horses' hooves were striking, leather straps were creaking, armor and swords were clanking all inside their heads, interspersed with sounds of heartbeats and the whistle of cold air passing through the nostrils.

"At least it isn't raining!" Fleance shouted over the clatter of the footfalls.

"But it will!"

Then Fleance saw something across the road ahead, a rope, or . . . no, it was chain, half concealed in the dirt. "Father, stop!" he yelled.

As Fleance spoke the chain rose out of the sand and snapped taut across the road.

"They are on us!" yelled Banquo. He jerked his horse's reins, but it was too late. His horse ran into the chain, tripping and falling, sending Banquo to the ground.

Fleance was able to turn his horse away just in time, but he circled back to see two men descending on his father, still trapped beneath his horse.

"Get the boy!" shouted one of the men to the other.

"Fly!" yelled Banquo. "Fly. It's too late for me!"

"Father!"

"Aaaaaaaaah!"

Blood flew in great arcs as a man plunged his dagger into Banquo's throat, then into his head and chest, over and over again. Fleance drew his sword and prepared to fight.

"Guh." Banquo mewled. His body was already limp. "Go. Go."

"No more out of you!" said one of the men. He grabbed Banquo by the beard and sliced his neck from ear to ear.

Fleance's horse reared as the other man leapt at him from behind. Fleance spun his horse around and brought the hilt of his sword down on the man's head. He was about to dismount and kill him when, in a moment of clarity, he remembered his father's words. Protect yourself. Flee. Ride home. Don't look back. He must have had a good reason for saying that.

Fleance spurred his horse. It leapt forward just as the other man lunged at him with a dagger. The blade cut the horse's thigh, but the wound only made it run faster.

"Don't let him get away!"

Fleance didn't look back. He heard no horses, but still he rode on as if all hell were chasing after him.

When Fleance reached the river fifteen miles away, he stopped. Only then did he realize what had happened. His father must have known. He knew the ambush would come. He knew and laid down his life to save his son.

Chapter Eighteen

The three witches stood at the cauldron muttering strange words when a spark—like a firefly—floated down from a storm cloud and hovered above them. It zigged and zagged, darting from one witch to the next. The first witch whispered something to a toad she kept in a pocket of her cape, whereupon it leapt after the spark, trying to snare it with its sticky tongue. Another swatted at the dancing light with her staff, and the third witch was about to throw her cloak over it when the spark burst like a firecracker. Out of the flash stepped a tall woman with a face as white as marble beneath hair as slick and black as the feathers of a crow.

"It's Hecate, our mistress!"

"Why do you look so angrily at us?"

"Why?"

"Why?"

The goddess scanned her surroundings with slow, unearthly movements of the head and eyes, like a mantis or a strange fish of the deepest, darkest ocean.

"Have I not reason? Witches as you are?" Her voice was singsong. "Saucy and overbold! How did you dare to trade and traffic with Macbeth in riddles and affairs of death? And I, the mistress of your charms, the close contriver of all harms, was never called to bear my part or show the glory of our art?"

The three witches hung their heads, afraid to speak.

"And what is worse," Hecate said, "all you have done has been but for a wayward son, spiteful and wrathful, who—as others do—loves for his own ends, not for you! But make amends now. Get you gone, and at the pit of Acheron meet me in the morning. Thither he will come to know his destiny."

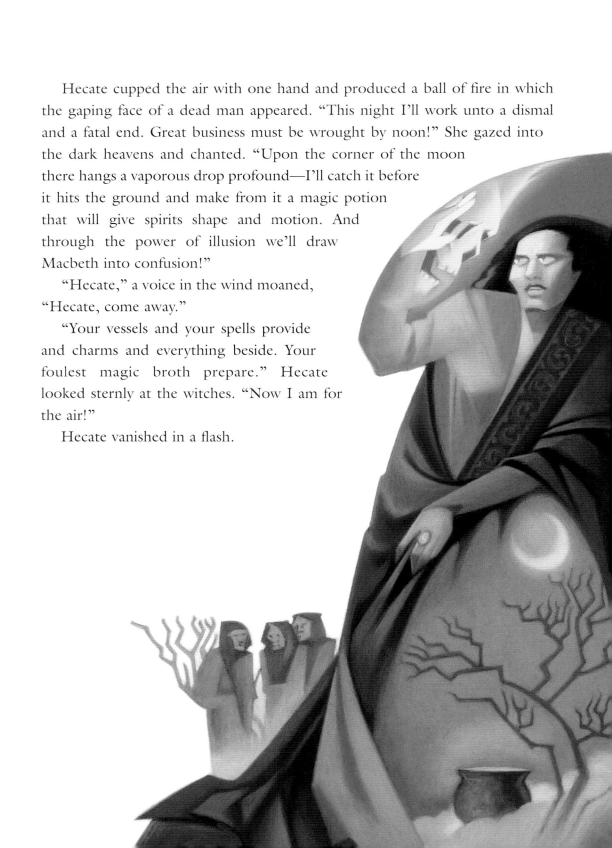

Hecate cupped the air with one hand and produced a ball of fire in which the gaping face of a dead man appeared. "This night I'll work unto a dismal and a fatal end. Great business must be wrought by noon!" She gazed into the dark heavens and chanted. "Upon the corner of the moon there hangs a vaporous drop profound—I'll catch it before it hits the ground and make from it a magic potion that will give spirits shape and motion. And through the power of illusion we'll draw Macbeth into confusion!"

"Hecate," a voice in the wind moaned, "Hecate, come away."

"Your vessels and your spells provide and charms and everything beside. Your foulest magic broth prepare." Hecate looked sternly at the witches. "Now I am for the air!"

Hecate vanished in a flash.

Chapter Nineteen

Lady Macbeth drifted between the tables in the great hall at Dunsinane Castle, watching the servants lay out the pitchers and the trays, the place settings, cups, and napkins. She was never one to take much interest in this kind of activity, and she wasn't any more interested in it now that she was the Queen. And yet she was the Queen, and her role was to be the center of the kingdom's social world, to lay out cheerful tables at cheerful parties, to be the charming dove flitting from one table to the next, ensuring the pleasure of her guests.

As she watched the tables fill up with roasts and pies, a thought gripped her that being queen amounted to no more than this silly show of hospitality. Was it for this, she thought, that I risked so much?

Mercifully the guests began to arrive, and she didn't have to think about it anymore.

"You know your places," boomed Macbeth as he ushered in Lennox, Ross, and several other noblemen and their attendants. "Take your seats. There is plenty for all. Our queen has seen to that."

"Yes." Lady Macbeth smiled as convincingly as she could. "You are all welcome."

The guests seemed even less at ease than their hostess. Each looked around the room, as if he might be taking note of the exits, and found a place.

From the kitchen door a servant gestured to Macbeth.

"Entertain them, my lady," said Macbeth. "Don't wait for me! Eat while I see to this business."

Entertain them? Lady Macbeth felt sick again.

In the kitchen, Macbeth was greeted by one of the men he had hired to kill Banquo. "Your Majesty," he said without bowing.

"There's blood on your face," Macbeth said distractedly.

The man wiped his face on his sleeve and examined the blood. "Banquo's," he said.

"Better on your face than in his body."

"My lord, his throat is cut. That I did for him."

"And Fleance?"

"Escaped."

Macbeth became dizzy. "Here comes my fit again." He sat on a stool. "Otherwise it would have been perfect . . ."

"But Banquo is dead, like you asked."

"Thanks for that," said Macbeth. "At least that means I'm safe for a little while. I should be happy."

The murderer shrugged.

"But that isn't your concern. Now go. You've done your part."

Lady Macbeth came in just as the murderer left. "The guests await you," she said. Then she saw how pale he was. "What's wrong?"

"Nothing," said Macbeth. "I am just hungry. Yes. Nothing's wrong that good food won't fix."

Lady Macbeth followed her husband back into the hall, where none of the guests had so much as picked up a fork.

"What?" said Macbeth. He still felt dizzy but tried to disguise it. "This doesn't seem like much of a feast. Where is the laughter? Where is the cheer?"

"We were waiting for you, my Lord," said Ross.

"Right," said Lady Macbeth. "What kind of party can it be without the King?" She took her place. "Sit and eat with us, or our guests might think this is an inn and expect a bill."

"Ha-ha-ha-ha!" Macbeth laughed more heartily than the joke warranted. It did little to brighten the dismal atmosphere of the miserable hall.

Macbeth stopped laughing and scanned the room.

"Sit, my lord," Lady Macbeth said.

Macbeth wobbled like a tree about to fall. "Where?"

"Um . . . here, my lord. In your place."

Macbeth looked at his chair next to his wife and saw Banquo, his face bloody and broken, his throat slashed.

Macbeth shook. "Which of you has done this!"

"What, my lord?" said Lennox.

Macbeth pointed at the grizzly corpse. "Who put that there?"

"The King is not well," said Ross.

"You can't say I did this!" Macbeth raged. "I was here the whole time!"

Then the corpse shook its head slowly, grinning.

"Don't shake your gory locks at me."

"I think it is time for us to leave," said Lennox.

"No," said Lady Macbeth. "Sit. The King is often like this—ever since he was a child. It is a momentary fit. Ignore him and it will go away."

Macbeth covered his eyes. Lady Macbeth rushed to him.

"Are you a man?" she hissed in his ear. "This is the very painting of your fear, like the air-drawn dagger you say led you to Duncan. These flaws and starts would well become a woman's story at a winter's fire! Are you not ashamed? There is nothing there but a stool!"

"Don't you see him?" bellowed Macbeth.

The guests began to make their way discreetly to the door.

"If you can nod your head, you might as well speak!" said Macbeth. "Tell all!"

The corpse vanished. Macbeth collapsed in his wife's arms.

She pushed him back on his feet. "My noble Lord, the guests are leaving."

"He was there," said Macbeth. "I saw him."

Lennox and Ross, who had kept their places throughout, listened to Macbeth's words with great interest.

"I don't understand," Macbeth mumbled almost incoherently. "Blood has been shed before now. In the old days, murders too terrible to be spoken of were performed all the time. Huh! Back then when you knocked a man's brains out, he'd stay dead. But nowadays, you stab a man twenty times and he comes back all bloody and won't even let a fellow sit down at his own dinner table."

"Heh-heh." Lady Macbeth tried to smile, but it was more of a wince. "As I said, he gets like this. Ignore him."

"A murder, you say, my lord?" said Ross, stroking his beard.

"I am sure His Majesty meant nothing," said Lennox, kicking Ross under the table.

"Meant?" said Macbeth, realizing at last what he had almost confessed. "What did I say? Don't look so surprised. I have a condition. It happens. Forgive me if I alarmed anyone."

"Of course," said Lennox.

"That's a relief." Ross grinned. "For it would not be believed that His Majesty had murdered someone."

Lennox kicked Ross again and took another look at the exits, happy that he had kept a dagger tucked in his stocking.

"So," said Macbeth, "now that it's over, let's have a toast. Everybody take a glass. Fill them up. Let's drink . . ."

"To His Majesty," said Lennox.

"To Banquo," said Ross. "And where is Banquo?"

"To Banquo? Yes." Macbeth nodded frantically. "Yes. We miss him. Good Banquo. Everybody drink to—Aaaaaaaahhhhhhh!"

The corpse came back, walking this time. It stepped up to Macbeth and looked at him through its blood-caked hair.

"Get out of my sight!" screamed Macbeth, dropping his glass.

Lennox and Ross got up.

"Stay, lords," said Lady Macbeth. "It's nothing."

"All the same, lady," said Lennox. "His Majesty is obviously distracted."

"Yes," said Ross, "it is best that he be alone during these fits, lest he say something that will make the people uneasy."

They hurried away with their attendants.

Macbeth rolled on the floor, blubbering. "Come as a bear, a rhinoceros,

a tiger—take any shape but that! Or be alive again! Be alive again! Hence horrible shadow! Unreal mockery! Go! Go!"

The corpse vanished again.

"The whole party has broken up," said Lady Macbeth. "And I fear you've said too much."

"You amaze me," said Macbeth. "How can you behold such sights and keep the natural ruby of your cheeks when mine are blanched with fear?"

"What sights? There was nothing here."

"'Blood will have blood,' they say, 'Blood will have blood,'" said Macbeth.

"You aren't making any sense."

"No? Then tell me, where was Macduff tonight, eh?"

"What are you talking about?"

"Macduff? Why is he not here?"

"I don't understand."

"Don't you? Oh, I hear the rumors. Ha! He is gone to—shhhhhhhhhhhhh." Macbeth put a finger to his lips. "England. But I keep a servant in his house, and he'll call on him soon enough. Yes, I am so deep in blood that it is just as easy to keep swimming to the other side as it is to go back."

Lady Macbeth gleaned the meaning of her husband's rambling words, and she didn't like it.

"You're going to kill . . . Macduff?"

"Shhhhhhhhhh! Strange things I have in head that will go to hand."

"My lord," said Lady Macbeth, "you must sleep."

"Sleep? No. I must go to the weird sisters. I must learn more, for good or for ill."

"You must sleep."

"No sleep."

"My Lord."

Macbeth stood. His eyes were wild. He began to walk away.

"Husband!"

"Shhhh!" said Macbeth. "I know what I must do. You sleep. I will take care of everything."

Chapter Twenty

The three witches stood in a circle around the stinking black pot, watching the pitch sputter and ooze.

"Thrice the brindled cat has mewed," said one.

"Thrice and once the hedgehog whined," said another.

"Round about the cauldron go," said the third, "in the poisoned entrails throw. Toad that lurks beneath cold stone, days and nights has thirty-one, sweltering venom sleeping got, boil first in our magic pot!" She plopped a dead toad into the broth.

Then all three chanted, "Double, double toil and trouble! Fire burn and cauldron bubble."

Another witch pulled out a bag full of bugs and innards. "Fillet of a fenny snake, in the cauldron boil and bake. Eye of newt and tongue of dog, adder's fork and blind-worm's sting, lizard's leg and owlet's wing, for a charm of potent trouble like a hell-broth boil and bubble!"

"Double, double toil and trouble! Fire burn and cauldron bubble."

"Scale of dragon, tooth of wolf." The witch dropped the objects into the pot as she spoke. "Maw and gut of salt-sea shark, root of hemlock dug in the dark. Finger of a baby smothered in a ditch by his own mother. And now about the cauldron sing, like elves and fairies in a ring."

"Double, double toil and trouble! Fire burn and cauldron bubble!"

"Shhhhh." The witches stopped their work.

In the distance came the sound of horses.

One of the witches brushed her fingertips together.

"What is it, sister?"

"Sister, what?"

"By the pricking of my thumbs, something wicked this way comes."

The hoofbeats came closer.

It was Macbeth.

Chapter Twenty-One

"How now, you secret, black, and midnight hags," said Macbeth, dismounting. "What is it that you do?"

"A deed without a name," the witches said in unison, their voices echoing each other.

Macbeth thought he heard a child's laughter in the wind as the witches spoke. A chill came over him. He began to speak, nearly shouting, as if he were trying to silence his fears and the raging storm at once. "I order you, by the magic you profess—however you came to know it—to give me answers to the questions I ask!"

"Speak."

"Demand."

"We'll answer."

The witches waited.

The courage Macbeth had talked himself into began to fade. He said nothing.

"Maybe you'd rather hear from our masters' mouths than from ours?" said one of the witches.

Our masters? Macbeth knew what he was being asked. He was already in so deep, did it matter . . . He could hardly finish the thought. Did it matter if he were giving his permission to call forth . . . devils?

"Call them," said Macbeth. "Let me see them."

One of the witches took the blood of a sow that had eaten her own piglets and mixed it with the fat of a dead man cut down from the gallows. She poured it into the cauldron, and out leapt a green flame, in the center of which appeared the face of a man wearing a hood of mail.

"Macbeth, Macbeth," the face said. "Beware Macduff."

"I knew it!" said Macbeth, "but tell me—"

The face vanished.

"He cannot be commanded," said the witch. She sprinkled some dust into the cauldron, and again the green flames shot out.

This time a bloody child appeared.

"Macbeth, Macbeth," it said, "be bloody, bold, and resolute. Scorn the power of man, for none of woman born shall harm Macbeth."

"Huh!" Macbeth laughed. "Then why should I fear Macduff? Though maybe I should kill him just to be sure. Do you think—"

"Listen!" said one witch.

"And speak not!" said another.

Then, without any prompting, a third vision appeared. It was a handsome young boy wearing a crown.

"Be lionhearted," it said. "Macbeth shall never vanquished be until great Birnam wood to high Dunsinane hill shall come against him."

The child vanished.

"That shall never be!" Macbeth roared. "Who can impress the forest, bid the tree unfix his earth-bound root?" But then his fear returned. "Though, I wonder, will Banquo's offspring ever be kings of Scotland?"

"Seek to know no more," said the witches, again in unison.

"No," said Macbeth. "All these predictions mean nothing if this one is true. Will Banquo's descendents wear my crown?"

The witches looked at one another and smiled.

"Show!" said one.

"Show!" said another.

"Show!" said the third.

And then they all chanted, "Show his eyes, and grieve his heart. Come like shadows, so depart!"

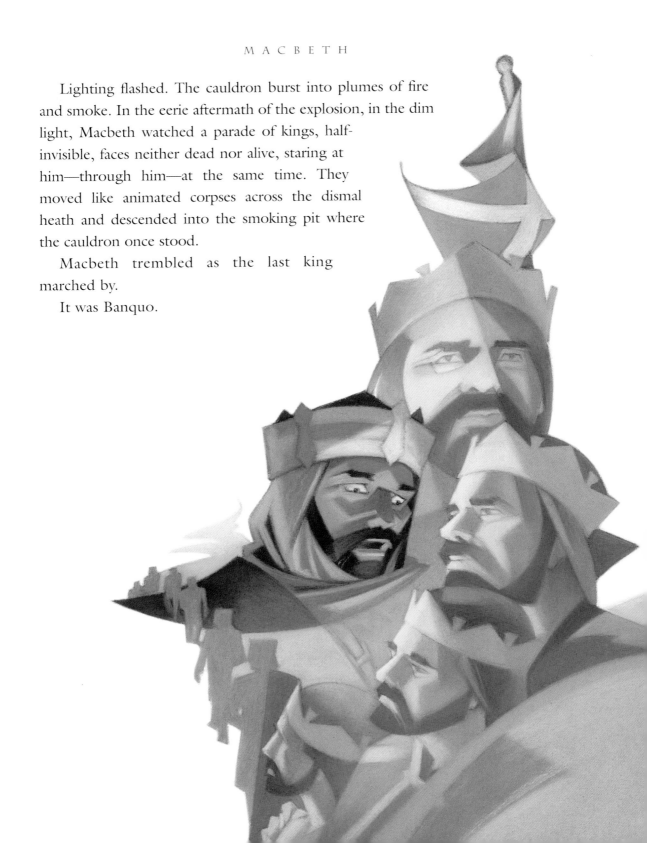

Lighting flashed. The cauldron burst into plumes of fire and smoke. In the eerie aftermath of the explosion, in the dim light, Macbeth watched a parade of kings, half-invisible, faces neither dead nor alive, staring at him—through him—at the same time. They moved like animated corpses across the dismal heath and descended into the smoking pit where the cauldron once stood.

Macbeth trembled as the last king marched by.

It was Banquo.

Chapter Twenty-Two

Ross had ridden hard all day. He had made a difficult decision and one that put him in great peril. Rumors were posting over the land. Macduff had gone to England to rally forces behind Malcolm. Ross took the occasion of Macbeth's secret errand on the heath to sneak away to Fife, to warn Lady Macduff of the imminent danger to her husband—and maybe to herself as well. He hoped he could get there in time; maybe he could even get back to Dunsinane before Macbeth condemned him as a traitor, too.

Although he suspects that everyone in the kingdom would be condemned as a traitor eventually, to a tyrant, everyone is an enemy but himself.

When he arrived at Fife, he found Lady Macduff in her upstairs chamber, nearly hysterical.

"Why has he run away?" she said. "Why has he left us? He has all but confessed himself a traitor by this cowardly flight."

Evidently, Macduff had spared his wife the truth about the state of the kingdom. Ross was reluctant to undeceive her, but he saw no alternative. "It is perhaps wisdom, Madam, not cowardice," he said.

"Wisdom? To abandon his wife and children? He loves us not, or else he wouldn't leave us here as traitors to bear the wrath of the King. Wisdom?!"

"He is wise, Madam, and noble." Ross lowered his voice to make sure Macduff's young son could not hear. "I dare not speak much further, but cruel are the times when we who know the truth and act upon it are made traitors. We are all floating upon a wild and violent sea now. We must move as we can. Your husband is doing nothing less by going to England, nor I by coming here. We are trying to save the kingdom and not destroy it."

"Is this true?" she said.

"Aye, Madam."

"Then we are all dead," Lady Macduff said. "All of us. There is no safeguard against a wicked king."

"Maybe there is," said Ross. "Sir Knight!" he called to Macduff's son. "It's time for you to be a soldier and protect your mother."

The boy ran forward with a wooden sword drawn. "I am ready!" he said.

"That's a brave fellow!" Ross looked at the little boy, no higher than his mother's waist.

"What can he do?" said Lady Macduff.

Ross whispered. "Not even a madman would kill a child in front of his mother or a mother in front of her child. Be brave."

Lady Macduff said nothing.

"What is he so afraid of, Mother?" said the boy, once Ross had left.

She stroked his hair. "He fears your father is dead," she said.

"My father is not dead for all your saying, Mother."

"Oh? I think he is," said Lady Macduff, trying to be strong. "You will have to think now about what you will do without a father."

"Well, what will you do without a husband?"

"Why, I can buy me twenty at any market, but we only ever have one father."

The boy thought for a moment. "They say my father is a traitor, Mother. Is that true?"

"Yes," she said. "That is what they say."

"And what is a traitor?"

"One who makes promises and lies."

"And what happens to traitors?"

"They are hanged."

The boy thought again. "But who hangs them?"

"Honest men."

The boy seemed confused.

"Does it not make sense that honest men should hang traitors?"

"Well," the boy said, "but there are more liars than honest men in Scotland, if what I have heard is true. So why would the liars let just a few honest men hang them?"

How deeply corruption seeps into a kingdom, Lady Macduff thought. She smiled and stroked her son's hair again. "God help you, poor monkey."

And then a crash came from the gates and then another and another. Lady Macduff knew what it was. They were breaking in the doors. They were coming.

"Run," she said. "Run!"

Footsteps clamored on the staircase.

"No, Mother," said the boy, "I will stay here and fight the honest men!" He held out his wooden dagger.

Into the room rushed a thin, rangy man with a leather coat and a scarred face. He was followed by soldiers.

"Stand!" said the boy.

The murderer kicked the boy in the face, sending him and the dagger flying across the room.

"Will you kill the—"

The man plunged his sword into the boy's heart.

"What has happened to my country?" cried Lady Macduff. "You will kill a child here in his mother's bedroom? A child? What has happened to Scotland?"

The man didn't answer but with one rough movement slashed his sword across Lady Macduff's neck.

Chapter Twenty-Three

Dunsinane Castle was in a frenzy. Macbeth had returned, his eyes wild, speaking strange words. There was to be war; that much was certain. But against whom? He spoke about England, about Macduff, about Fleance, and about Malcolm. He also spoke about witches and midnight and ghosts. The enemy seemed to be everywhere and nowhere, faceless and without substance, but close and subtle, at least to the King.

The alarm had rung unendingly. Horses were fitted with armor. Carts were loaded with provisions and gunpowder. The armory had been turned out, and every man and boy who could carry a sword had two. The captain of the guard tried to ready the men, but he didn't know himself where they were marching or against whom.

"Quickly," roared Macbeth, "quickly!"

"My Lord," said the captain, "where shall we tell the men we are going? We need to prepare them."

"Going?" said Macbeth. "Nowhere. Here we shall make our march and our stand."

"Our march? Our stand?"

"Don't look so stupidly," said Macbeth. "My orders are clear enough. This shall be our battlefield."

"Dunsinane?"

"Yes, Dunsinane. This is where we shall win our victory. This is where we shall keep the kingdom safe. Or do you think we need more world than this?"

"But who is the enemy, my Lord? Who is invading?"

"I haven't time for this. The enemy is everywhere." Macbeth pushed past the captain. "Ross!"

A hush fell.

"Ross!"

"Ross has not returned," said the captain.

"Good," said Macbeth. "Another traitor gone. Hang them all. Listen!" he shouted. "If there are any other traitors here, you can leave. This is Scotland. Where I stand is Scotland. If you don't believe that, and if you are not ready to die here, then I don't need you! Who wants to leave?"

It crossed the captain's mind to raise his hand.

"Lennox!"

"He's gone, too, Your Majesty."

"Better," said Macbeth. "I don't need him either. Send Ross to me."

"Your Majesty?" said the captain.

Macbeth glared. "What?"

"Ross has, eh, gone, as I said. No man of note is here but Your Highness."

"Oh." Macbeth's dizziness returned. "That's good. Yes. That's good. Great men are dangerous, not to be trusted. Remember that if you are ever King of Scotland. Get rid of the great men first. Nothing but trouble."

The soldiers listened to the madness of their king and commander, but buried their thoughts in their tasks. What else was there to do?

Chapter Twenty-Four

"Ross!" said Macduff, leaping to his feet as his old friend came into the tent.

"Well met," said Ross gravely. "And greetings to you, my lord." He bowed to Malcolm.

"What news?" said the prince.

"The tyrant is arming himself in a blind rage. He is friendless but fearless, and driven by strange beliefs he keeps to himself. Has anyone heard from Fleance?"

"He is safe. He has joined my brother Donalbain, newly landed in the west from Ireland. They stand in reserve."

"We will win," said Macduff.

"Yes," said Ross, "but we have already lost so much."

"It can be repaired. A nation heals," said Malcolm, "when it is ruled honestly."

Ross bit his lip.

"But there is something you are not saying," said Macduff.

"I wish there were not."

"Come," Macduff said. "I have already guessed at it. Tell me."

"Your castle," said Ross. "Fife. It was surprised."

Macduff nodded. "And what price does the tyrant ask for my family? Unconditional surrender?"

"No price, Macduff. There is nothing that can ransom them."

Malcolm put his hand on Macduff's shoulder and left the two old friends alone.

"Are they . . . dead?" said Macduff.

"Aye. They killed her. And your children. Servants. Anyone who could be found. I had just left."

"Dead? My children? My wife? Dead?"

"I am sorry."

Macduff just stood there, speaking without thinking. "Dead? All my pretty chickens? Dead? And their mother?" Then he pounded the table with his iron glove. "Oh, hell-kite! Only a man with no children could do it!"

"We'll find a way to pay him in kind."

Macduff's rage turned back again to disbelief. "I cannot remember a time when such things were. Dead? Did not the heavens intervene on their part? I must have sinned dreadfully." He began to cry. "How can this be? How can the world have turned into this?"

"Let your grief be the whetstone of your sword," said Ross. "Convert it to anger."

"Convert?" said Macduff. "There is no difference between grief and anger when all is taken away. Loss is felt only when something is left to measure it against. I have nothing, nothing but anger. Dead. All of them." And then he clutched Ross's arm. "Promise me, when the time comes, you will let me kill him."

Chapter Twenty-Five

"How long has she been like this?" the doctor whispered.

Lady Macbeth walked as if in a trance up and down the gloomy torchlit hallway, rubbing her hands.

"Ever since His Majesty went to the field," said the Queen's lady-in-waiting. "Many times I have also seen her rise from sleep, go to her table, write a letter, and fold it up, all fast asleep."

"A cruel trick of nature," said the doctor, "to sleep without rest."

He scrutinized the ghastly expression on the Queen's face and the frantic way she rubbed and rubbed her fingers. He had heard the rumors.

"Let me ask you this," he said, in a very low voice. "Has she said anything?"

Fear spread across the face of the woman. "I would not repeat what I have heard without another witness to confirm it," she said, "though it is nothing that the wind itself does not cry out."

"I see." The doctor understood. "And you say she will abide no darkness?"

"Aye," said the woman. "It is as if she were a little girl, terrified of the night. I don't doubt she has reasons."

Lady Macbeth stopped for a moment and held her hand up to the light. "Here's a spot," she said. She licked the corner of her sleeve and began to rub her palm with it.

The doctor quietly withdrew a slip of paper from his coat. "I think we should write this down."

Lady Macbeth finished rubbing the phantom spot on her palm and seemed for a moment satisfied. But then she looked at her other hand. "Here's another," she said, and began to rub. "And another." She was rubbing her hands, her wrists, her arms. "And another. Out, damned spot! Out, I say!" She knelt and scoured her hands against the apron of her gown. "Ha. Hell is murky. What are you afraid of, my lord? You're a soldier. What? Afraid of a little blood? Why, who cares who sees it when no one has the power to punish us?"

The doctor wrote it all down.

Lady Macbeth examined her hands and smiled, as if they were clean.

"Yet who would have thought the old man had so much blood in him?"

The doctor scribbled, not believing what he heard and yet knowing, as everyone in Scotland did, that it was true.

As Lady Macbeth stared at her hands, her smile faded. "Blood," she said. Her voice became dark and husky. "The Thane of Fife had a wife. Where is she now?"

"Oh, no." Her lady-in-waiting bit off a cry. "No." It was too much to bear. It was said Lady Macduff had been slain in front of her own child, or her child in front of her. Was her Lady, the Queen, party to a crime that went against nature itself? Could she have bathed and dressed and cared for . . . a monster?

"What?" said Lady Macbeth. "Will these hands never be clean? No more of that, my lord, no more! You'll ruin everything with these fits of yours." She stood then walked gracefully across the room and held her hand out to the mirror as if she were offering it to her own reflection for a kiss. "What? The smell of blood's here still? Of course it is, my dear. All the perfumes of Arabia will not sweeten this little hand."

She clutched her breast and began to sob.

"This disease is beyond my practice." The doctor tucked the paper away, and he and the waiting woman tiptoed toward the door.

Lady Macbeth wheeled around and jabbed a finger at them. "Put on a nightgown and come to bed, I say! Banquo is buried. He cannot come out of the grave!"

Lady Macbeth didn't see them go.

Alone she stared at her finger, still outstretched. "Give me your hands, I said." And she cupped her hand and held it to her chest. "It's time for bed, my little one. Shhhh. My pretty babe. Shhhh. What's done cannot be undone. Shhhh."

Chapter Twenty-Six

Macbeth stood on the battlements and stared out into the endless gloom. All around the walls his soldiers and archers waited at the ready. They had been waiting for days, silently. He had all but forgotten they were there. They were visions, half-real, like ghosts, and their vague and soundless presence made him feel that much more alone.

But he didn't need anybody. He repeated the words to himself. None of woman born shall harm Macbeth. Macbeth shall never vanquished be until great Birnam wood to high Dunsinane hill shall come against him. He was invincible, for every man was born of woman, and a forest could not move. But . . . why fear Macduff? Why had the spirit said that? He pondered all the different things these words could mean, coming up with nothing certain.

He used to ask his wife about such things, but there was no use talking to her anymore. For all her courage and willingness to act, she lacked the stomach to follow through. She understood murder, yes, but so does every criminal. It takes a great man to understand and accept that every murder doubles itself—for every man you kill, you have to kill two more. Doubling, doubling, one, two, four, eight. Anyone could kill, but not everyone could keep killing.

That is why I am King, he thought, and took courage from his wisdom.

But still he wondered why he should fear

Macduff. And whether Banquo's children really would become kings.

"Your Majesty?" came an apprehensive voice, the captain's.

"What is it, cream-faced loon?" Macbeth said, sorry to have his thoughts interrupted by a human presence.

"There are, my lord, 10,000—"

"Ten thousand geese?" said Macbeth.

"Soldiers, sir."

"Well, are they geese or soldiers?! Make up your mind." Macbeth stormed over to the bewildered man. "For if they are soldiers, then unless they were somehow born without women, I couldn't care less. And if they are geese, then tell the cooks that we will feast tonight."

The captain knew it was futile to reason with the King, who had obviously lost his mind, but he felt he had to say something. "Your Majesty, your people are frightened. They have not slept or eaten. And the gloom of this ancient fortress weakens even the bravest heart. Please, I beg you, speak some encouraging words to them. They know the English forces are afoot."

"How about this," said Macbeth haughtily. "None of woman born shall harm Macbeth. What more is there to know?"

"What about the harm that may come to them? What can you tell your people to give them hope and courage?"

"You can tell them that if their whey-faces cannot bear the heat of battle, then they can die!"

"Very well, Your Majesty." The captain bowed and left.

"And bring me no more reports of soldiers or geese!" Macbeth shouted after him.

He resumed his watch on the battlements. A few minutes later, the gates of the castle creaked open, and some sixty men scurried away, some dragging their families.

Macbeth had a mind to order his archers to shoot them down, but what was the use? It didn't matter if he had a million men protecting him or none. There weren't enough arrows to kill all those who wanted to run away from him.

He paused for a moment on this last thought and remembered a fantasy

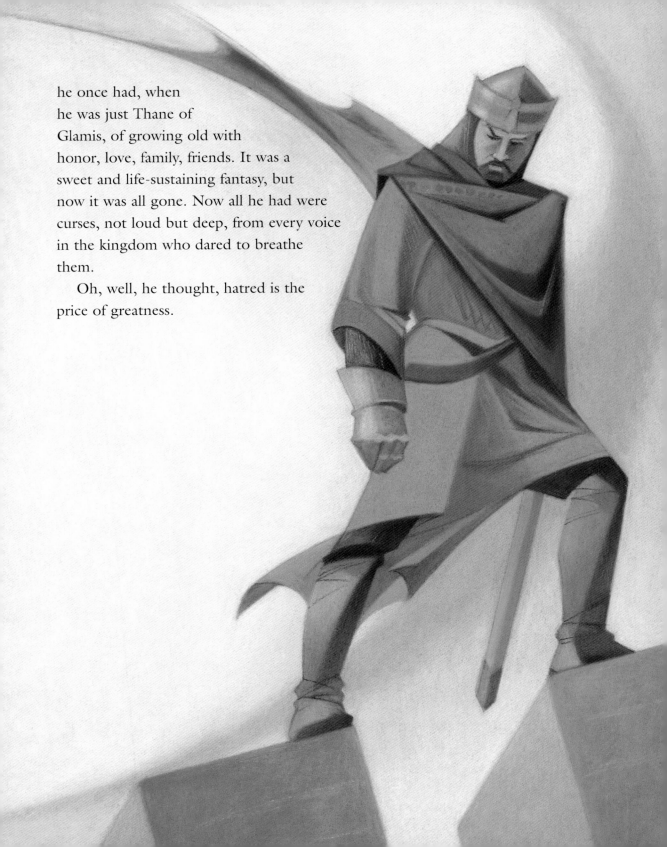

he once had, when
he was just Thane of
Glamis, of growing old with
honor, love, family, friends. It was a
sweet and life-sustaining fantasy, but
now it was all gone. Now all he had were
curses, not loud but deep, from every voice
in the kingdom who dared to breathe
them.

Oh, well, he thought, hatred is the
price of greatness.

Chapter Twenty-Seven

Lennox spurred his horse onward to the appointed place, his cavalry rolling behind him. He left Donalbain at the coast and took the cavalry and half the Irish infantry with him to meet up with Malcolm, Macduff, and Ross, who were riding northward from England. A messenger reported they were well past the Tweed and marching hard for Dunsinane. As confident as he was of their chances, he was not naïve as to what kind of battle lay in store for them. Crazy and friendless as he was, Macbeth was a formidable warrior, still the greatest in Scotland. He wouldn't be put down easily.

Ahead he saw the vanguard, with Ross at their head.

"Whoaa!" he called to his horse and rode forward with a few of his officers.

"Well met," said Ross.

"Aye," said Lennox. "Does everything go as planned?"

"We come with 5,000 on horse and 500 more afoot. English and Scottish. Malcolm, Macduff, and Fleance each lead a regiment. With your forces we will hit Dunsinane from each side." But Ross was not naive either. "And what intelligence do you have from Dunsinane?"

"The tyrant has strongly fortified it. Some say he is mad; others that hate him less call it valiant fury. Either way, he is out of control. His forces every day run from him, and it is said he laughs at their defection."

"What else can he do but laugh?" said Ross. "Now he feels the secret murders sticking on his hands. He can only command, for none love him. He feels his title hang loose about him, like a giant's robe upon a dwarfish thief."

"Aye," said Lennox. "With some luck we'll put an end to it soon enough. Where shall we rally the forces?"

"I have surveyed the battlefield and recommend Birnam forest. We can conceal ourselves there and rest before the assault."

"Good," said Lennox. "Then I will meet you there. Give the Prince and those noble Scotsmen he commands my sincerest greetings."

The two friends shook hands and rode off.

Chapter Twenty-Eight

"Open the gate!" cried the captain.

The portcullis rumbled up as a soldier, desperately clutching the reins of an exhausted horse, rode through.

"Where are the others?"

"Gone." The soldier fell out of the saddle and tried to stand. "We were surprised."

The captain gave him a flask of water. "Did you see the English forces?"

"Not clearly." The soldier drank deeply and spat. "How many they were I could not determine. But they encamped in Birnam forest."

"Who said Birnam forest?" Macbeth pushed his way through the crowd. "What about it?"

"Your majesty forbade me from giving any new reports about the English forces," said the captain.

"But what about Birnam wood?" Macbeth lifted the soldier and shook him. "It isn't moving, is it?"

The soldier was confused. "Moving, my Lord?"

"Aye, moving. Moving! Can you not hear?"

"Your Majesty," said the captain.

"I said is Birnam Wood heading this way or not!"

"No, my lord," said the soldier. "It's . . . right there . . . in Birnam. Though it now contains some 15,000 soldiers preparing to attack us."

"Let them prepare. We have nothing to fear as long as the forest stays where it is."

The soldiers looked at one another, each wondering why they had not fled Dunsinane when they had the chance.

"Why are you all so linen-cheeked?" said Macbeth. "They can't harm me."

"We can't repel such a force," said the captain.

Macbeth whirled around and struck the captain down with his gauntlet. "The next man who says we can't or we mustn't dies! Let the battle come. Let the bloodshed begin. When the battle is over, Scotland shall belong to the bloodiest and the bravest, no matter how many soldiers the English have. Is that understood?"

"Yes, my lord," said the captain, regaining his feet. "We shall try to be bravest and I am sure we will be bloodiest, when all is done."

"My Lord." It was the doctor. "A word with you."

"To your stations," said the captain, and the crowd departed, leaving Macbeth alone with the physician.

"What is it?" said Macbeth.

"Your wife, the Queen."

"What about her?"

"She is troubled with thick-coming fancies."

"Well, give her something," said Macbeth, climbing the stairs to the battlements.

"My Lord, they do seem to flow from some secret lodged in her heart."

Macbeth stopped in his tracks. He turned to the doctor, expecting to see in his eyes the accusations of a traitor, yet another person trying by force or guilt to snatch away his hard-bought kingdom. But what he saw were the gentle eyes of a caregiver.

Macbeth sat on the step. "Cure her of that, can't you?"

"Therein must the patient minister to himself," said the doctor gently.

The subtle accusation jarred Macbeth out of his momentary remorse. "Throw medicine to the dogs," he said. "I'll have none of it." He stood up and tightened his armor. "Doctor, the captains and thanes fly from me, and I am left alone to defend Scotland. If you are a physician, then examine my kingdom and find her disease. Get some rhubarb or purgative drug that would make her vomit these English forces hence. Have you heard of any such remedies?"

Macbeth drew his sword and shut his visor with an ominous clank.

The doctor did not miss the implied threat in the King's gestures. "Seeing Your Majesty preparing for battle is cure enough for me," he said.

"I thought it might be. Now, enough of this talk. And enough of this waiting for time and destiny to unfold. I want this war to begin!"

Chapter Twenty-Nine

The battle cries from Dunsinane echoed over the heath and penetrated Birnam wood.

"What's that uproar?" said Ross.

"Maybe he's decided to make war on himself," said Lennox. "He must be running low on enemies by now."

"Then let's give him an enemy," said Macduff. "Let's charge him now. He's too weak to defend Dunsinane against us."

Malcolm considered the opinions of his generals. True, Macbeth was out of his mind and his forces were weak, but that also meant he had nothing to lose. "Too risky," he decided. "He has worked the castle into a frenzy. We should attack when their blood is cold, not when it's hot."

"We can't wait here forever," said Macduff.

Malcolm knew Macduff was right. Their supplies and the morale of the soldiers would diminish every minute they lay hidden in Birnam wood.

"I also worry that the open field between the edge of the wood and Dunsinane is too long," said Lennox. "If we attack, we are sitting ducks for his archers."

"What about this," said Malcolm as the idea struck him. "Birnam wood is just close enough to Dunsinane that it is visible and yet far enough away that its details cannot be descried, especially in this gloom. What if every man in our force cut limbs from the trees and concealed himself?"

"Ah!" said Ross. "And we could march on line—disguised as trees. We would be halfway to Dunsinane before Macbeth knew we were even there."

"Three-quarters of the way, in this gloom," said Lennox. "And we could

move our batteries forward behind the line of trees. I like it. We would still have to charge through the open field, but the distance we will be able to travel in relative safety will spare many, many lives."

"Give the order," said Malcolm. "Every man must conceal himself. Even us."

Macduff listened patiently. He knew the plan was sound, and yet one thing still gnawed at him. "This is all fine," he said. "But remember, I have asked that you let me kill Macbeth myself."

The others did not argue with him.

Chapter Thirty

Macbeth surveyed the field from every angle, and still there was no sign of the English force. Just the gloomy heath and the thin line of trees in the distance. It is a siege, he concluded. The army of the traitors is lurking in the woods. Let them lurk, he thought. Let them lurk until famine and ague eat them up.

His own soldiers held onto the walls like drowning men clinging to spars. Fatigue and hunger were eating them, too. How long they had stood there waiting without relief he no longer knew. It didn't matter. His destiny was fixed, and the lives of the men around him were only part of his destiny. They would suffer and die—or not—according to his fortune. The wheel of the world turns around the king. If ordinary people were crushed under that wheel, such was the way of things.

He smiled. For the first time since snatching away the crown, he felt like a king. He had thought he would have felt it before, during the coronation ceremony and the triumphal march, but parades and ceremonies were just show, and nothing made one feel less a king than performing for others. Now it was the sheer loneliness that confirmed his kingship. He moved through a world of silent forms, where no one understood him, no one questioned him, no one challenged him, no one even spoke to him. Cut off from humanity, isolated in his mind, he felt as if he were the one thinking and acting man in a universe of powerless shadows.

But his reverie was broken by a cry.

What is that noise? he thought.

The cry was followed by another and another, women's voices, shrieking in terror and grief.

The captain ran toward him, his face pale and his lips trembling.

Macbeth studied the captain with more fascination than fear. How funny, he thought. I have almost forgotten the taste of fear. Once my senses would have cooled to hear a night-shriek, and my hairs would have stood on end as if they were alive. But I have dined with horrors. There is nothing the night or terror itself can do that is more horrifying than my own thoughts.

"Did you not hear a scream, Your Majesty?"

"Is that what it was?"

"My Lord—"

"Whatever it is, it doesn't concern me."

"The Queen, my Lord, is dead."

"She would have died tomorrow if not today."

As soon as he uttered the words he felt the force of their meaning.

"My Lord?"

Macbeth said nothing as the reality of his situation made itself clear in an instant. Ever since he had murdered Duncan and seized the throne, there was nothing left to hope for other than that his crime would not be discovered and that he would be king another day. Nothing would come tomorrow or the next day or the next that was better than the present. Human beings cannot live that way. We need to hope; we need something to look forward to. We need to believe that with the progress of time we will grow into something more than what we are. For the world will change, and we will change whether we want it to or not. If we can find nothing hopeful in those changes, life is impossible and pointless.

So the Queen might as well have died today, thought Macbeth, for her future was a blank, as mine is.

"Your Majesty?" said the captain.

Macbeth slumped against the wall.

"Bring the doctor!" shouted the captain.

Macbeth paid no attention but stared into the feeble light of the torches burning on the battlements. "Tomorrow and tomorrow and tomorrow," he said, "creeps in this petty pace from day to day until the last syllable of recorded

time, and all our yesterdays have but lighted fools the way to dusty death. Out," he snuffed out one torch with his iron glove and then another. "Out, brief candle. Life's but a walking shadow, a poor player that struts and frets his hour upon the stage and then is heard no more. It is a tale told by an idiot, full of sound and fury, signifying nothing."

"My Lord!" It was not the doctor but a messenger.

"Speak quickly," said Macbeth.

"My gracious Lord," the messenger said, panting, "I should report that which I saw but know not how to do it."

"Well, say it."

"As I did stand my watch upon the hill I looked toward Birnam, and . . . I thought the wood began to move."

"What?" said the captain.

"Liar!" shouted Macbeth. "Liar and slave!"

"Within these three miles may you see it coming," the messenger gasped.

"If you speak false, you shall hang alive upon the next tree till famine cling thee," Macbeth raged. "But if it is true—" Macbeth made a noise between a laugh and a sigh. "I know nothing anymore, except the double talk of the devil, who lies like truth. Fear not till Birnam wood do come to Dunsinane? And now a wood comes to Dunsinane. There is no escape now. I begin to grow weary of the sun."

"Then we will surrender, my lord?" said the captain, who wondered what sun his king had grown weary of—since it had not been seen in days.

"No," said Macbeth. "I will play out the scene. Nothing I do can alter destiny."

From out on the heath the sounds of trumpets erupted. The charge was sounded.

Chapter Thirty-One

"Throw down the branches!" shouted Malcolm. "Make the trumpets speak! Give them all breath!"

With a deafening shout 10,000 men threw down their camouflage and stormed toward Dunsinane as the trumpets blew.

Lennox and Ross spurred their horses. Malcolm rode forward in front of the standard-bearer. Macduff dismounted and charged on foot, leading the infantry forward. Behind the charge the pipers filled the air with a steady drone that could be heard even above the tumult of war.

"Now!" shouted Macbeth. "Now we will win or lose all!" He rushed from station to station along the castle walls as his soldiers boiled oil and prepared their arrows. He saw the terror in the eyes of the men. But in his mind they were dead already, so it didn't matter.

At that moment a stone the size of a barrel, hurled from a catapult, crashed into the west turret of Dunsinane Castle, shattering it like glass. Another flew in, missing its mark and landing in the courtyard, but a third struck right above the main gate, cracking but not destroying the ancient stone.

"Arrows!" shouted Macbeth. "Shoot!"

More stones flew in and the arrows began to whir through the air.

Lennox could barely feel the pounding of his horse's hooves against the earth, could barely see his way through the haze. All around him were the screams of the dying, but still he rode on. He looked to his left and saw Ross, galloping over the bodies of fallen soldiers on his way to the castle walls.

Macduff stepped quickly but carefully through the confusion, his eyes on the top wall of Dunsinane Castle. Every man he saw looked like Macbeth. He couldn't wait.

Malcolm charged forward, and the standard-bearer came fast behind him. He watched the massive stones battering the castle. Soon it would be time to put up the ladders, and then the real battle would begin. He watched the arrows stream in like rain against the castle and as many fly out from the cracks and apertures in the walls.

Still the pipers played.

"My Lord! We cannot hold back their numbers!" shouted the captain as the first ladder struck against the castle walls.

"Then die!" said Macbeth. He split an English soldier in half and pushed the ladder back to the ground.

But more ladders sprang up. And still more. Until every man on the battlements was slashing wildly at the Englishmen who scrambled up.

"How stand the gates!?" yelled the captain.

"Holding!" cried a sergeant who, along with thirty other men, were pushing against the splintered doors. "But not for long."

"Damn the gates!" said Macbeth. "Let them come!"

"Booooom!" A horrible explosion came from the east turret. A soldier there, the last of the detachment tasked with holding the tower, had touched off a powder keg, taking his own life but destroying more than a dozen English soldiers who had overrun his position.

"Promote that man!" said Macbeth. He whirled along the castle walls, hacking off heads, hands, and arms, indifferent to his own danger.

"My Lord, we cannot hold out!" The captain beat back an invader. But it was too late. The English overwhelmed him. A mace crashed down on the captain's helmet, and man after man swooped over the wall.

"The doors are open!" a sergeant called as the English pushed through the splintered gate.

"Enter the castle!" cried Malcolm over the confusion.

Lennox and Ross turned their forces toward the main gate, their work on the ladders having been accomplished. Ross had taken an arrow just under his armpit. He was weakened but not undone. Lennox was somehow unscathed, although he had lost his horse. They charged toward the battle standard waving above the yellow smoke that clung to the battlefield.

The forces pushed and hacked at the splintered oak doors until they fell off their hinges. A shout went out and they poured into Dunsinane.

Macduff continued his slow, inexorable pace, taking no chances. He had prepared himself this day for one great task and one task only, and he wasn't going to let a stray arrow deter him.

Macbeth lifted his visor and watched the English soldiers cut through the few men left standing on the battlements. He watched more English soldiers stream in through the hole in the castle wall where the gate used to be. Those not yet dead were surrendering; those not surrendering were put to death.

One thought gave him some hope, if hope is what he wanted. The witches had told no lies so far, which meant no man born of woman could harm him. With that thought and the strength he still possessed, he lowered his visor and prepared for his final battle.

"Who's he that was not born of woman?" he yelled.

No one came forward. Macbeth's strength was legendary. Even though there were men enough to overtake him, nobody wanted to go first.

"Just put an arrow in his heart!" said a voice in the crowd.

"Yes," said Macbeth, "but be quick. The tyrant is almost upon you." His blade made an evil hiss as he swung it in the air.

Lennox and Ross pushed their way to the front.

"Traitor to Scotland," said Ross, "you should die like a dog!"

"Then kill me like one, if you can."

Lennox very nearly drew his sword, but he remembered the promise he and the others had made to Macduff.

Macbeth kept moving forward. Men scrambled to get out of his way.

If Macduff didn't show up soon, thought Lennox, they would have to fight

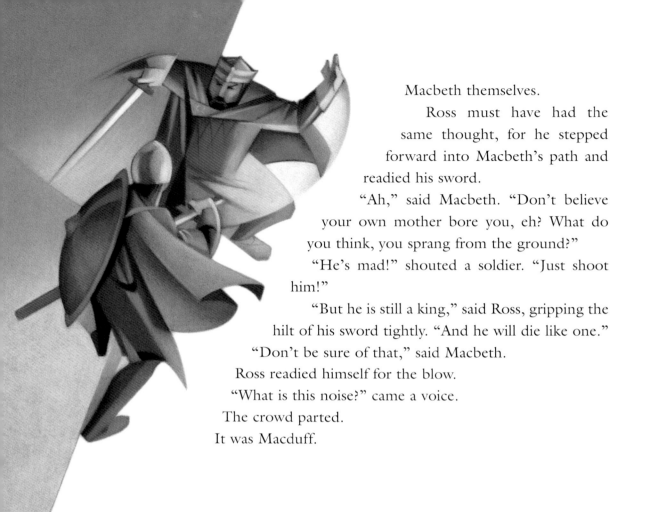

Macbeth themselves.

Ross must have had the same thought, for he stepped forward into Macbeth's path and readied his sword.

"Ah," said Macbeth. "Don't believe your own mother bore you, eh? What do you think, you sprang from the ground?"

"He's mad!" shouted a soldier. "Just shoot him!"

"But he is still a king," said Ross, gripping the hilt of his sword tightly. "And he will die like one."

"Don't be sure of that," said Macbeth.

Ross readied himself for the blow.

"What is this noise?" came a voice.

The crowd parted.

It was Macduff.

Chapter Thirty-Two

Macduff stepped slowly toward Macbeth. "Good thing you're still alive," he said. "If you die by some other sword than mine, my wife and children's ghosts will haunt me still."

The words of the witches rang in Macbeth's ears as Macduff drew his sword. "Beware Macduff . . . None of woman born shall harm Macbeth." Now here was Macduff, but he had to be of woman born—everybody was. So which prophecy was right?

"Of all men I have avoided you," said Macbeth. "But stand back—I already have too much of your blood on my soul."

Macduff thought Macbeth was taunting him. "Then I should say you will go that much deeper into hell when I send you there, but I have no words for you. Let this sword speak for me."

"Let it be quiet." Macbeth raised his sword. "You will waste your labor and your life."

Macduff did not listen. He rushed at Macbeth and delivered blow after furious blow, all of which Macbeth easily parried.

Finally, when Macduff had exhausted himself, Macbeth spoke. "As easily may you make me bleed as the impervious air. Go find someone else to kill. I lead a charmed life, you see, which cannot yield but to one not of woman born."

Macduff smiled. Then he laughed. Then he laughed some more. He rose to his feet, rejuvenated. He looked into Macbeth's distant eyes and spat. "Your charm is over," he said. "Go back to your witches and ask them, if you doubt what I am about to say is true. I'll wait!"

Macbeth didn't ask what he meant, for he knew. "You—"

"Yes," said Macduff. "I was from my mother's womb untimely ripped."

"Damn these fiends!" said Macbeth. "Damn them all, who palter with us in a double sense, who keep the word of promise to our ear and break it to our hope. I'll not fight with you."

Macbeth dropped his sword.

"Then yield to me, coward," said Macduff, "and live to be the show and sensation of the age!" He laughed again. "We'll make pictures of you—and write on them 'Here may you see the tyrant' so that everyone who does not believe they exist can see one!"

As sad as he was and as much as he suspected his end had finally come, Macbeth was not ready to throw himself on the mercy of the country he had abused. "I will not yield to kiss the ground before the feet of Malcolm or Fleance and be baited with the rabble's curses. No. Though Birnam wood has come to Dunsinane and you stand before me as one not of woman born, yet I will try to my last breath." He stooped and picked up his sword. "Lay on, Macduff!"

Macbeth rushed forward, but the charm had ended. Macduff timed his strike perfectly, swinging his blade cleanly through Macbeth's neck.

Chapter Thirty-Three

Trumpets sounded. Macbeth watched three figures appear in the hazy frame of the open gate, and for a moment he thought they could be the witches. But he knew, without understanding why, that the witches were gone. Their work was done. The figures he saw were bright. The sun glinted off their armor and illuminated the gold and red of their hair. Behind them banners flew, white crosses on a field of blue, and behind them were the green hills of Scotland dotted with purple flowers.

The figures came closer and Macbeth recognized them as Malcolm, Donalbain, and Fleance. They smiled at him. How long had it been since anyone was happy to see him? He tried to speak but he couldn't, tried to say how lucky Scotland was to be delivered into the care of such worthy young men, tried to say, somehow, that he was sorry.

Then he felt himself falling.

"Behold," said Macduff, "the usurper's cursed head." He threw Macbeth's head to the ground at Malcolm's feet. "I see you compassed with the kingdom's pearl. I speak with the voice of all the people when I say hail, King of Scotland!"

And then the whole castle shouted, "Hail, King of Scotland!"

Malcolm closed Macbeth's eyes and covered the head with his cape. "We must mourn all we have lost and repair the kingdom before we can celebrate," he said. "My brother Donalbain, worthy Fleance in whom I see the future of the kingdom shining like a star, Ross, Lennox, and you, Macduff, bravest of all, I proclaim you thanes no longer but earls, the first Scotland has ever known.

And I charge you with spreading the news of this fair day so that all our exiles will return home and every Scotsman will know that this butcher, his fiendlike queen, and all their ministers of tyranny are dead."

None in the crowd listened more solemnly to the words of the new king than Fleance. The rumor of the witches' prophecy had reached his ears, and as he stared at the bloody lump beneath Malcolm's cape he warned himself never to forget how easily a good man can become a tyrant, especially when half-truths play on fantasy and ambition.

If it could happen to Macbeth, he thought, it could happen to anyone.

"Now," said Malcolm, "let us go to Scone so that the crown may pass to its rightful heir according to our custom."

"Long live the King!" shouted Fleance.

"Long live the King!" shouted Ross and Lennox and Macduff until the whole castle rang with the cheer. The kettle drums began to quake, the trumpets sounded, and the newly made earls followed their king out of the castle.

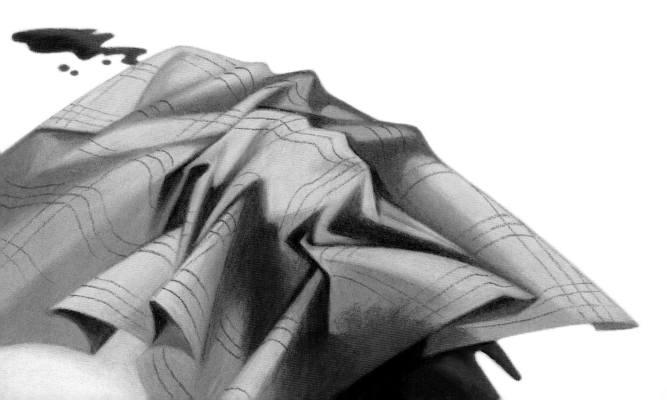

QUESTIONS PEOPLE ASK ABOUT
MACBETH

Why is *Macbeth* sometimes called "the Scottish play"?
Legend has it that this play is cursed. Many actors and stagehands have reportedly met with inexplicable accidents during productions over the years, and so it has become a tradition among theater people to avoid its real name.

If Duncan is the king why does he have to name his son Malcolm as his successor? And why then wouldn't Macbeth also have to kill Malcolm and Donalbain, Malcolm's brother, in order to be king?
The crown in ancient Scotland did not pass automatically to the eldest son of the king, as it did in England, but, by mutual agreement, to the worthiest of the noblemen. Duncan is, therefore, out of order by naming his son to the throne without the proper consent of the thanes.

Does it help me to know anything about the place names in this play—like Scone, Dunsinane, and Inverness?
Not really, but you can still go see the castles (or, in the case of Dunsinane, the ruins of a castle) at these locations in Scotland.

Is there any significance to the ingredients of the witches' magic potion that's boiling in the cauldron?
Yes and no. No, in that none of these items contains any special properties that we know of, but yes, in that people of Shakespeare's time generally thought they did.

Who is Hecate?
In Greek mythology, Hecate (pronounced HEK-a-tee) is the goddess of magic and sorcery.

What is "the pit of Acheron" that Hecate talks about?
The Acheron is the "river of woe," one of the five rivers of Hades, the Greek underworld. Sometimes Acheron is used to refer to Hades itself, as it is here.

Why can't they just shoot Macbeth with an arrow?
According to tradition, kings and other noblemen had to be killed nobly, by sword and not by other means. Even in the case of an execution, one would behead a nobleman not with an axe but with a sword. In practice, however, war has probably never observed rules of decorum. We know, for instance, that Sir Philip Sidney, one of the most esteemed gentlemen and writers during Shakespeare's time, died unceremoniously from a gunshot wound while fighting against the Spanish.

Should it be Birnam wood or Birnan wood? I have heard both.
Some editions of this play say "Birnan wood." Most modern publications of Shakespeare plays are made from consulting various older printings, most of which are flawed in some way. (Shakespeare, you will recall, never oversaw the complete publication of his plays.) Many of these older printings disagree, as is the case of Birnan versus Birnam wood. Probably Scotsmen in 1606 would have called the forest near the ruins of Dunsinane castle "Birnan wood," but a number of early editions of *Macbeth* say "Birnam wood," and since this spelling is more familiar to most readers, I have left it that way in this book.

Why isn't the prophecy fulfilled at the end of the play? Why is Malcolm, not Fleance, the new king?
Shakespeare's audience would have known that Fleance was supposedly King James's ancestor, and so the prophecy within the play is fulfilled by James himself.

WHO'S WHO IN
MACBETH

MACBETH:	Thane of Glamis and Duncan's chief general; later Thane of Cawdor and King of Scotland
LADY MACBETH:	Macbeth's wife
BANQUO:	Macbeth's friend and another of Duncan's generals
FLEANCE:	Banquo's son
DUNCAN:	King of Scotland
MALCOLM:	Duncan's son, Donalbain's brother
DONALBAIN:	Duncan's son, Malcolm's brother
MACDUFF:	Thane of Fife
LADY MACDUFF:	Macduff's wife
LENNOX:	A trusted nobleman
ROSS:	Another trusted nobleman
DOCTOR:	Macbeth and Lady Macbeth's personal physician
CAPTAIN:	Macbeth's chief officer at Dunsinane
THREE WITCHES:	The weird sisters
HECATE:	Goddess of magic and witchcraft

INDEX